MILE HIGH ADDICTION

ZARA COX

Boldwood

First published in 2013 as *High*. This edition published in Great Britain in 2025 by Boldwood Books Ltd.

Cover Design by Judge By My Covers

Cover Images: Adobe Stock and iStock

A CIP catalogue record for this book is available from the British Library.

Paperback ISBN 978-1-83678-897-3

Large Print ISBN 978-1-83678-896-6

Hardback ISBN 978-1-83678-895-9

Ebook ISBN 978-1-83678-898-0

Kindle ISBN 978-1-83678-899-7

Audio CD ISBN 978-1-83678-890-4

MP3 CD ISBN 978-1-83678-891-1

Digital audio download ISBN 978-1-83678-893-5

This book is printed on certified sustainable paper. Boldwood Books is dedicated to putting sustainability at the heart of our business. For more information please visit https://www.boldwoodbooks.com/about-us/sustainability/
Boldwood Books Ltd, 23 Bowerdean Street, London, SW6 3TN

www.boldwoodbooks.com

To my beautiful, greedy book besties who want it all: a furnace-hot, angst-ridden billionaire who gives good grovel and greater orgasms, this one is for you. xoxo

1

The first thing Bethany Green saw when she opened her mailbox on Friday evening was the indigo-colored envelope. Against the rest of the junk mail and bills, it stood out like an exotic jewel in the dust.

Even as she cautioned herself against excitement, her heart skipped several beats. Fingers trembling, she reached for the rectangular envelope and felt it, real and heavy in her hand.

"Omigod, it came. It actually came." Realizing she was talking to herself, albeit in the empty foyer of her apartment building, she quickly stuffed the mail in her oversized handbag and hurried to the elevator.

She'd barely stabbed the button for the fourth floor before she pulled the envelope out again. The words written on the front in raised gold embossed lettering were simple—Your Invitation. She turned it over. No return address. No surprise there. Because, seriously, only a crazy person would turn down this invitation.

Ten minutes later, Bethany, despite being fortified with half a glass of Rioja, still hadn't gathered the courage to open it. The harsh buzz of her cellphone made her jump. Unable to tear her gaze from the envelope, which now rested on her coffee table, she fumbled on the sofa for a few seconds before her fingers closed over her phone.

"We still on for tapas in an hour, right?" Keely Benson, her best friend, snapped in her no-nonsense Brooklyn twang.

Keely was pure New Yorker, not an up-stater like Bethany. Many times during their long friendship, Bethany had thanked God for having Keely in her life. She'd been there for her when Bethany had been hit with the worst news of her life.

"Umm... yeah... I guess," Bethany replied, her attention still absorbed by the envelope.

"You... guess? How many times over the last week have I told you how important tonight is to me? Fuck, Bethany, if you chicken out on me, I'll never forgive you. You know Clark will never go all the way if I come on too strong. I need you to pull me back. Once I get him to my place, I'll be fine, but I can't have him wimping out on me at dinner, and for that to happen, I need you there!"

"Jesus, Keel, I've never understood your insane addiction to nerds."

Her friend gave a rich laugh that started off as a schoolgirl giggle and ended in a dominatrix's growl. Bethany had seen grown men drool like little boys when Keely laughed.

"You don't need to understand, baby girl. All you need to do is to turn up and help a friend out."

"I... Okay, sure, I'll be there."

Keely huffed with impatience. "Okay, tell me what's going on. You haven't had another run-in with She-male, have you?"

Bethany smirked at the nickname they'd coined for her balls-shriveling boss. "No, she's out of town till Tuesday."

"Then what the hell's the problem?"

"It came," Bethany blurted out, incapable of keeping the news to herself any longer.

"It? What it?"

"An invitation. To The Indigo Lounge."

Silence. For as long as Bethany had known her, Keely had never been at a loss for words. For her to be silent now made Beth's heart hammer. Her friend knew, just as she did, the gravity of the moment.

"You're. Shitting. Me!" she finally whispered.

"I am not." A sound bubbled up from Bethany's throat—half incredulous, half terrified. Because she still couldn't believe what her eyes were telling her.

"Have you opened it? What does it say? When do you leave? How long for? Are you allowed to bring a guest? Fuck it, girl, spill!"

"I… haven't opened it yet. And, seriously, Keely, I don't think I want to."

"You don't think you want to open it or you don't think you want to accept the invitation?"

"Umm… both? I mean, there's no way I can get away on such short notice. Besides, I have too much work to do at the moment. June is our busiest month because it's right before everyone disappears for the summer… It's just not practical—"

"Bethany!" Keely's steely voice cut across hers.

"Yes?"

"How much wine do you have at your place?"

Bethany finally managed to blink and focus on something other than the indigo envelope. Glancing over at the alcove set into the short hallway leading to her kitchen, she counted. "Three reds, one white, one rosé. Why?"

"I'll be over in twenty minutes. I'll bring takeout."

"What about Clark?"

Keely sighed. "As much as it kills me to deny myself some super-hot nerd cock, Clark can wait. This is way too important to let you do what I know you're thinking about doing."

"But—"

"Twenty minutes." She hung up.

Bethany forced herself to breathe. Willed her hands to stop shaking. Taking another sip of wine, she picked up the invitation.

The Indigo Lounge—owned by thirty-one-year-old billionaire Zachary Savage, the fifth richest man in America.

The piece she'd read about Savage in *Time Magazine* last year had expounded on his Midas-touch business savvy and hinted at his rags-to-riches background, but she'd known the report was largely rehashed from other articles. The very private Zach Savage had revealed almost nothing about his past to his interviewer.

The picture used in the piece had been an old one from his post-college years, but it didn't detract from the fact that at twenty-five, Zachary Savage had been magnetic and gorgeous, with eyes that captured and held a woman's attention and made her want to get to know the man behind the enigmatic, sexy smile.

Nowadays, all anyone knew about Zachary Savage was that he lived somewhere on the West Coast, probably San Francisco, owned several homes around the world, and had fingers in multiple entrepreneurial pies, the most renowned being The Indigo Lounge.

Operating from ten super-jumbo private jets, the lounges offered prime, private adult entertainment. Rumors said they were flying sex palaces, but the specifics were an extremely well-kept secret that only the cream of A-listers were familiar with.

The events organizing company she worked for had made

overtures for his business last year and been met with a flat refusal. Bethany, as part of the bidding team, had been tasked beforehand with finding out everything she could about Zachary Savage.

Coming up near-empty had more than pissed off her bosses and made her position at Neon Events, Inc. precarious. She'd had to work her ass off after that debacle to redeem herself in the eyes of her immediate supervisor, Sheena Malcolm.

The sound of her buzzer interrupted her thoughts. Springing to her feet, she buzzed Keely in and waited by her front door.

Her blonde, green-eyed friend exited the elevator with her usual brisk, sexy stride, carrying a takeout bag from their favorite Chinese place in one hand and two Louis Vuitton weekenders in another.

Bethany frowned as Keely walked past her into the apartment. "What are the bags for?"

Keely dumped the luggage on the floor next to the nearest sofa and headed for the kitchen. "One is empty and is for you to use once I convince you you're going on this trip. The other is for if I've lost all my powers of persuasion and I don't succeed. In which case, you and I are taking off for the Hamptons for the weekend. The weather forecast says mid to high nineties. If I won't be sweating it out on my sheets with Clark, I might as well go sweat on a beach and top up my tan while we discuss the serious issue of how you live your life." She grabbed two plates and came back into the living room where she'd left the food on the small dining table tucked into a corner and started dishing out Kung Pao chicken and noodles.

Bethany stemmed the fierce reaction to the word beach and tried to hide her fear-induced shudder. Keely saw it anyway.

Sympathy softened her gaze. "Crap. Scratch the beach idea.

In fact, scratch the whole contingency plan. You won't be needing it."

"Actually, about the invitation..."

Keely grimaced and pointed her chopsticks at her. "You've talked yourself out of going, haven't you?"

"I don't think I can take the time off work, Keel."

"Sure you can. Your Aunt Melanie has suffered her second heart attack in two months. All those donuts and greasy short ribs the doctors warned her about are finally taking their toll. They don't know if poor Aunt Mel will make it this time."

"Jesus, Keely, Aunt Mel is as healthy if not healthier than the horses she rides several times a day. I spoke to her on her birthday last week and she's as fit as a fiddle."

"Iron Balls Sheena doesn't know that. She's approved you taking all of the vacation time you've accrued in the last two years to visit your aunt's death bed in Montana. And..." Keely fished her cellphone out of a pocket and waved it at Bethany. "She just texted me back to say she's also happy for me to keep her updated so you don't need to check in every fucking day."

Bethany couldn't stop her mouth gaping. "You packed a bag, ordered food for us and texted my boss asking for time off all in what... twenty minutes? Just so I'll go on this trip?"

"Yup."

"And Sheena believed the excuse you made up?"

"Why wouldn't she? She still thinks I quit Neon last year because she drove me to a nervous breakdown and not because Rubio Events poached me. Bet she's scared spitless I might sue her ass." Keely grinned and handed over a steaming plate. "I love it when you get that look on your face."

"What look?"

"The one that says you don't know whether to kiss me for

coming through for you or bitch-slap me for grinding your excuses into dust."

"Yeah, because I've learned to my grief that when you're this determined, one of us ends up doing something she'll regret. And most of the time, it's me."

Keely waved her away and went over to the sofa Bethany had vacated minutes earlier. She stared down at the envelope with the same awe Bethany had felt since opening her mailbox almost an hour ago. "Wow. I mean... fucking wow."

Bethany released a shaky breath and felt a little better that she hadn't blown the epicness of the situation out of proportion. "I know, right?"

Keely nodded. "We still need to open it, babe. We're not going to get the juicy details by staring at it all night." With a deep breath, she snatched it off the table and ripped it open.

Bethany held her breath until the need for oxygen made her inhale greedily. "What does it say?"

"You're leaving on Sunday from Newark. First stop is Shanghai... You'll have your own personal guide, chef and a bodyguard throughout the experience... Holy crap!"

"Bodyguard? Why would I need—"

Keely held up a hand. "Second stop is Bora Bora. Jesus, Bethany, I'd kill to go to Bora Bora! Third stop, the Aleutian Islands—where the fuck are they?"

When Bethany shrugged, she continued. "Fourth stop London, fifth stop is Monte Carlo." She stared into space and sighed. "This is fucking unbelievable, Bethany. Did you think you'd hit the jackpot like this when you researched The Indigo Lounge and found out they take a wild-card guest once a year free of charge?"

"Nope. We both thought it was a joke at the time, remember?

I mean, what would a multi-billion-dollar organization have to gain from offering a once-in-a-lifetime opportunity like this?"

"Maybe Zachary Savage doesn't want the world to think he's just a super-rich dick?"

"Why should a guy who doesn't give personal interviews and is practically a recluse care what the world thinks of him?" Bethany asked.

"Jeez, I don't know. But let's not stare this gift heifer in the mouth." She pointed the edge of the envelope at Bethany. "This invitation has fallen into your lap, and you. Are. Going."

Bethany pressed her lips together to stop the torrent of objections rising inside her. On the one hand, she was thrilled—beyond thrilled. On the other, her self-confidence had taken a severe blow six months earlier when her long-term boyfriend had left her... for another man. Her shock at Chris's double betrayal still hadn't worn off. More and more lately, she was beginning to wonder if it ever would.

"What else does it say?" she asked to distract both herself and Keely from the reasons why taking this step felt so very daunting.

Keely glanced down at the envelope. "The usual disclaimers—total, unwavering confidentiality or you lose both kidneys, no drugs on board the jets... No drugs on board the jets... No drugs on board the jets or you'll be prosecuted... Jeez, they really hammer the 'no drugs' things home."

"Maybe someone had a bad experience with drugs on board?"

"Hmm... They have twenty-four-hour entertainment on board, but the private suites are private. Fuck, if you come back and tell me you never left your suite, I'll kill you." Keely glared at her.

"I haven't agreed I'm going yet, Keel."

Her best friend sighed and dropped the envelope. "Listen. I know why you don't want to go. Chris-the-A-hole did a real number on you with that I-prefer-men thing, I get that. Hell, it didn't even happen to me and I was fucking traumatized. But you need to move on, baby girl. You've worn out six vibrators in the last six months and God knows how many more dildos, and those are the ones you've told me about—"

"Keely!"

"You'll break your goddamn clit if you don't stop using battery-powered gadgets on it and believe me, you need your clit for when a real man comes along. Seriously, can you tell me you don't miss the real thing? A warm body against yours, a hard cock inside you?"

Heat suffused Bethany's face and she sagged onto the sofa. "Okay, fine, I do but—"

"No buts."

"Yes, buts! For fuck's sake, Keely. The last hard cock I had inside me decided it preferred anal with other men. It is any wonder I have a goddamn complex?"

Keely's green eyes gentled in sympathy. "Of course not."

"Those are stories we read in trashy magazines and laugh ourselves hoarse. Do you know how it feels to know I'm suddenly that girl? The one who couldn't keep her man happy enough, so he jumped into bed with another man?" Even after all this time, just saying the words made her stomach turn over with pain, anger and disgust.

Slowly, Keely shook her head, but then she got the look in her eye. The look that said, *I love you but...* "No, I don't know how it feels, honey, but neither am I going to let you hide away forever because of what that asshole did. What better way to get over it than to open yourself to new experiences? You go, you have a sizzling, no-strings-attached hook up in the lap of pure luxury, and you come back and move on with your life. Bethany, the Indigo Lounge couldn't be more perfect for you right now."

"It's not that easy..."

"Yes, it is. You need to get your ex out of your system, and a flying sex palace is just the way you're going to do it. You really should give up trying to fight me because I'm not letting you chicken out of this, B. It's time to step back into the real world." She picked up her dish and sat back, chopsticks poised. "Now eat up, you'll need your strength to keep up with the to-do list I've drawn up for you."

* * *

Sunday dawned bright and sunny over New York.

Bethany lay in bed, her whole body alert and tingling with an excitement she hadn't felt in a long time. It would've been the perfect time for a session with her Rabbit but Keely had confiscated each and every pleasure-giving gadget before her diva exit last night.

When Bethany had begged, she'd produced a brand new, hermetically sealed one, which was now stashed in one of the two large weekenders at the foot of her bed.

"You're not allowed to open it until after a full day on board the jet and only in case of emergency. And if you bring it back unopened, I'll love you forever."

Heaving a sigh of regret at the loss of Dildo Pete, Bethany got out of bed and jumped into the shower.

Twenty minutes later, Keely's super-aggressive revving of Bethany's beloved Mini Cooper, Hermione, made her wince.

"Please promise me you'll go easy on Herm while I'm away?"

"It's just a car, B."

They argued all the way to Newark Airport about Keely's

shoddy treatment of Hermione, but both fell silent when they drove into the private jet area of the airport.

The Indigo Lounge jet was immediately recognizable. The immense, gleaming black super jumbo jet with two thin lines of indigo running from nose to tail screamed its dominance over the smaller, lighter-colored planes.

Keely slowed as they gaped at the jet. "Color me sludge-green with envy. Remember you owe me one. I could've had Clark reciting the Fibonacci sequence to me while I fucked the living shit out of him Friday night and last night. Now all I have is nerd porn for company while I imagine you living it up on that jet. At least promise me you'll have wild fun?"

The look in Keely's eyes was a cross between that of a worried sister and a stern schoolteacher. She brought the car to a stop in front of a glass and steel building that had "The Indigo Lounge—Executive Guest Suite" over the doorway.

Bethany nodded. "I can't promise it'll be wild, but I'll have fun." She tagged on a smile and saw Keely relax a little—if it were possible for someone as high-strung as Keely to relax.

"Great, now... shoo!" Keely made accompanying gestures.

Bethany opened the door, stepped onto the hot asphalt, and smiled.

As she reached into the back where her bags were stashed, a gust of wind blew out of nowhere, lifting the skirt of her dress.

A low whistle sounded. "Christ, check out those legs."

Grabbing her bags, she turned to see three good-looking guys, dressed like they knew their way around the style section of a grooming magazine.

She heard Keely's satisfied laugh. "You're off to a great start, I see." Taking her sunglasses off her head, Keely jammed them on her face. "*Adios, amiga.*"

Bethany had just enough time to slam the door before Keely

accelerated away in a squeal of tires. Poor Hermione was in for a hammering. Trying not to wince at the fate of her car, she turned toward the Indigo Lounge office.

The men were disappearing into the glass building. She followed slowly, her pulse thundering at the knowledge that she was stepping over an unknown threshold. She glanced back at the huge black and indigo jet, a feeling of mingled apprehension and excitement shivering through her.

The opportunity of a lifetime.

She could shy away from it; from the possibilities of letting go and having... *fun*. Or she could embrace it in the hope that the experience would help her banish the pain of the past few months once and for all.

2

Zachary Savage looked up from the papers he was perusing and watched three men enter the Executive Guest Suite.

From his position behind the glass wall of the mezzanine floor office he'd commandeered from his assistant, he tracked them with narrowed eyes.

The lead member of the rock band Friday's Child was immediately recognizable. Back in what felt like another life, Zachary had attended a couple of their gigs. But that was before everything had gone to hell.

As usual, any thoughts of how his life had changed over the past six years made his jaw clench with anger and sorrow.

If he'd known that this stopover would clash with one of his Indigo Lounge flights, he'd have made other arrangements and placed himself very far away from harsh reminders of the past.

What the hell, he was here now.

That he normally did the guest vetting from the comfort of his San Francisco home office was neither here nor there. The stopover from London to refuel his jet was taking longer than expected. Working while he waited helped contain the restlessness that continued to prowl inside him.

He tried to get his brain back to work mode. So far he'd gone through the info on all the passengers boarding his plane except one.

As far as he'd been able to determine, the band members were clean. No evidence of drug use or excessive drinking. The other six parties travelling on this Indigo Lounge experience had been equally vetted. He tracked the band members to the front desk, watched them flirt with the receptionist.

Boredom escalating, his gaze returned to his papers. There was only one unknown quantity.

Bethany Green. The wild card.

Her invitation had been issued late, but so far the preliminary background check was clean.

He was about to flip over to the photograph page when a flash of yellow caught his attention.

She stood framed in the doorway of his building, two large weekenders clutched in her hand and an oversized purse slung over one shoulder.

Long dark hair spilled in rich waves around her bare shoulders and over her arms. Zach couldn't immediately see her face against the sunlit backdrop, but what he saw of her body made his breath catch as something flickered awake inside him.

The way she held herself intrigued him; slightly unsure but poised on the threshold, as if talking herself into taking the next step. In his world, women reveled in being ball-breakers, strove to show no weakness in his presence in hopes of impressing him.

Seeing a woman who recognized her vulnerability and struggled to own it was oddly captivating. He stood and walked to the window, surprised by how much he wanted to see this woman.

The wind caught and flattened her short dress against long, sexy bare legs, legs that seemed to go on forever before they curved to embrace rounded hips and a firm, flat stomach.

Zach's cock jerked, stunning the hell out of him with a hunger his jaded existence hadn't allowed him in a very long time. When his gaze reached her breasts, he let out a growl and realized his fingers were braced against the glass, his head almost touching it as he strained to see her face.

But she remained in shadow, poised on the threshold of the building, undecided whether to step in or bolt.

Come in.

He realized he'd whispered the words and froze, a touch of confusion making him frown. As he watched, her head cocked to the side, one hand lifting to brush her long, luxurious hair off her face. And still he couldn't see her.

But with her hair out of the way, he caught sight of a sleek neck, smooth skin.

The hunger grew, slammed inside him like a living thing. His cock, now fully awake, demanded action. Action it hadn't seen in weeks because even the thought of sex had bored him to distraction. Until now.

He breathed in deeply, every nerve in his body straining to see her fully.

Come in!

She continued to play with her hair, holding it back from her face. He grew harder, nearly dizzy with the force of his erection.

Finally, she stepped forward.

Zach's breath blew out of his body when he saw her face. Sensation hit him with the strength of a force-five hurricane. Her features were luscious; her pink mouth full and deliciously curved as if created for kisses... *his* kisses. High cheekbones and a pert nose completed the gorgeous tableau, and he watched with unwavering attention as she entered his domain.

With each step she took, he felt a powerful charge go through him. By the time she was directly below him, his fist was clenched against the glass, his emotions and his body both on fire.

She glanced up directly at him, but of course, she couldn't see him through the one-way mirrored glass. At that angle, her face was even more stunning, her clear blue eyes shining with a mixture of excitement and apprehension.

Zach wanted all her excitement and none of the apprehension. Hell, he wanted her, period.

No, "want" was too tame to describe the feelings coursing through him. The desperation churning inside him was as alien as it was forceful. He didn't do spontaneous. Didn't crave a woman on just seeing her. Nowadays, his girlfriends were carefully chosen, fully vetted.

And yet...

She lowered her gaze, shook her head slightly as if to clear it and looked around her. The moment he saw her head for the desk where the rock band were getting checked in, Zach cursed.

He was running out of his office before the string of filthy words was complete.

* * *

Bethany tried to shake off the strange sensation that had come over her and moved toward the front desk, where a drop-dead blonde goddess was checking in the last of the group of men. One of them, dark-haired and wearing an expensive-looking leather jacket, glanced over at her and winked.

She wasn't naïve enough to mistake his interest but her return smile felt strained all the same.

Now that she was here, out of the sphere of Keely's confidence, she was bombarded with second thoughts. And that sensation she'd felt a moment ago as she looked up at the frosted glass, the feeling like she was on a yawning precipice, staring into the face of danger... well, that had scared the shit of out her—

A door to the side of her burst open, and Bethany stopped dead.

Jesus!

He was all her wet dreams personified. The living god of her sexual fantasies, her daydreams and her cravings come to life.

Eyes the color of slate zeroed in on her from a face so incredibly stunning that her mouth went dry. His bold stare transmitted a raw sexual pulse of electricity straight between her legs. As he moved like an animal barely caged by civilization, her clit pulsed to life—contrary to Keely's hypothesis, it wasn't quite dead yet it seemed.

Everything fell away, every human being in the vicinity ceased to exist as she stared at the god before her. The vaguely familiar god...

His shoulders were wide, strong and imposing. He was breathtakingly tall, easily six-foot four, with hair as black as the T-shirt he wore with black jeans that emphasized narrow hips and taut, manly thighs.

Weathered boots and a chocolate-colored leather jacket completed the package but did nothing to disguise the air of raw masculinity that vibrated from him.

He stared at her as if he had the right to, as if he owned her and intended to claim her right there and then.

Bethany's pulse raced as she stared back, feeling extremely vulnerable but unable to pull her gaze away.

He moved one more step and stopped right before her, threatening to block out even the sunlight.

"Welcome to The Indigo Lounge."

His voice, like honeyed gravel, rough yet melodic, sent another wave of heat right through her.

Bethany had no trouble imagining it during sex, whispering hot, dirty things to her as he fucked her. God, he probably fucked like a goddamn champion.

What the hell had he said? Welcome?

"Umm... thank you."

He finally broke his electric focus and nodded over to a spare desk. As if conjured up by magic, another blonde goddess appeared behind it.

This one seemed to have eyes only for the man in front of her. No surprise there. But the avid interest in the woman's gaze made Bethany itch to wipe the smile from her face.

"Serena, can you check in Miss...?" He looked at her, one brow raised.

Bethany forced herself to focus. "Green. Bethany Green."

His eyes gleamed, then his lashes swept down to shield his expression. He nodded and turned to Serena. "Check Miss Green in, and arrange for my bags to be moved, too. I'm joining this I.L. trip."

Serena's eyebrows hit her carefully arranged bangs. "You're no longer heading to the West Coast?"

His nostrils flared slightly, and his jaw protruded as if he was battling with himself. Finally, he smiled. "No. Change of plan. Can I rely on you to arrange that, Serena?"

Of course he could. Serena's simpering smile indicated Mr.

Sex God could rely on her to arrange everything to suit him—including herself should the whim take him.

"Right away, sir."

Sex God smiled. "Not quite right away, Serena. First, please assist Miss Green."

Stormy grey eyes locked onto her once more. There was something about him that was so devastatingly powerful, Bethany had to force herself to look away, desperately willing her brain cells to track when Serena asked for her passport.

She handed it over, along with her copy of the Indigo Lounge agreement, which she'd signed in triplicate. All the while, the burn of his gaze silently branded her.

When Serena fake-smiled and handed back her passport, Bethany's hand shook as she placed it in her purse. The force of his stare was that little bit too much for comfort.

"If you leave your bags right here, they will be taken onto the plane. Your hostess, Tracy, will be here in a moment to introduce you to your team and she'll arrange the final search."

"Search?"

Serena's fake smile stretched wider. "It's our company policy to do a drugs search before our clients board. It's right there in the agreement you signed. Mr. Savage's rules about drug use on his planes are very strict."

Bethany's teeth ground together at the patronizing tone but she forced a smile. "Sure. If Mr. Savage insists."

"He does," Serena emphasized, casting another simpering look past her at the Sex God.

Bethany glanced over at him too and caught his faint look of amusement. But the moment their eyes met, the amusement faded, replaced by sizzling, possessive heat once more.

He shifted as if the same restless energy that prowled

through her stormed through him as well. His fingers flexed, then he jammed them into his back pockets. The movement stretched the material of his T-shirt over his powerful biceps, making her mouth water.

She struggled to rein in her reeling senses. She'd never felt like this before, not even with Chris—

Yeah... Chris. *Not thinking about him right now!*

"Allow me to escort you to your hostess," the man said, rocking forward on his feet.

She wanted to ask him who he was, why he was taking an interest in her check-in, but the chemistry between them was blatant enough, powerful enough, that words seemed superfluous.

Despite her floundering, despite the puzzlement as to why such a sexy and gorgeous man was watching her with barely contained hunger, she couldn't dismiss the bone-deep truth firing through her body.

Bethany wanted to fuck him. Pure and simple.

Except there would be nothing pure or simple about it.

The jaded wariness she saw in his eyes didn't detract from the raw sexual experience that lingered within the grey depths. Sex with this man would be insanely filthy; it would be nasty and sweaty. It would also be beautiful and complicated beyond words. She knew it as surely as she knew her own name.

Without answering, she nodded and fell into step beside him.

Behind her, Serena gushed about seeing to his needs, but neither of them paid her comments any attention.

His scent, warm, lemony with a hint of spice, filled Bethany's head along with a dizzying progression of filthy thoughts. God, she wanted to lick him in places she'd never once dreamed of licking a man! And that was just the beginning...

He led her through the doors he'd emerged from what felt like an eternity ago. A set of luxuriously carpeted stairs led to another door on the mezzanine level.

He stood to one side and waved her up, a wicked smile curving his sensuous lips. "After you, Miss Green."

Thank God she'd shaved her legs last night, was her first thought. Her second was whether her panties were visible through the thin fabric of the flirty yellow Vera Wang summer dress Keely had insisted she wear.

Oh, what the hell did it matter?

Propriety had gone out the window the moment she'd set eyes on this man. All the same, she couldn't stop her hand from fluttering against the back of her dress as she mounted the stairs.

She heard his soft hiss and belatedly realized that all she'd done was succeed in plastering the material against her ass. Her Kardashian ass, as Keely liked to call it.

By far it was her worst feature, ridiculously large in comparison to the rest of her body. While her breasts were an okay size, and her stomach and thighs having been primed with ballet from an early age responded well to exercise, her ass let her down every time. It was why she'd given up her dreams of becoming a prima ballerina.

She reached the top of the stairs and quickly dropped her hand.

Before she could open it, he reached past her and threw the door open.

The moment she entered, she knew why she'd felt the weird sensation as she'd walked into the Executive Guest Suite.

Moving forward, she stopped in front of the glass wall, her heart hammering wildly in her throat as she looked down into the open space below.

"You were in this room when I came in." It wasn't a question. It was another certainty that stemmed from her soul.

"Yes." His voice, hypnotic and sexy as hell, washed over her.

"You saw me."

"Yes." He was closer, close enough for her to smell him again.

"And you came downstairs?"

"I couldn't not."

She turned. He stood less than a pace away, those mesmerizing eyes on her. Again, his shoulders and his hands moved restlessly, as if he were physically restraining himself from touching her.

"So, what now?"

His gaze raked her from head to toe and back again. His lips parted and his tongue traced the inside of his lower lip. "Now you place your hands on the wall behind you and spread your legs."

Stunned excitement rocked through her, but she forced herself to breathe, to remain lucid. "W... why would I want to do that?"

His smile was filled with pure sin. "For your drug search, of course."

"What... what about Tracy?"

His smile disappeared. "She won't be conducting the search. I brought you here because now I've seen you, now I have you, Bethany Green, I refuse to let anyone else touch you."

He took that last step until they were a whisper apart. His head lowered and his nostrils flared as he breathed her in, the sharp tinge of need in his every exhale. "Are you ready?" he rasped.

She looked up at him, every nerve in her body tightening with need.

"No. You're about to put your hands on me and I don't even know your name."

"My name is Zachary Savage. You can call me Zach. In fact, I prefer it. Because Zachary is too long for the many times I intend for you to scream my name when I make you come."

3

Sweet. Baby. Jesus.

"I don't think you're allowed to say that to your guests, Mr. Savage." She was stunned that her voice sounded halfway normal because her brain was jumping with the shock of finding out who was stood in front of her.

Holy hell, she was talking to Zachary Savage! Although her brain had fired off that possibility when she'd first seen him, she'd discarded the idea because as captivating as the picture of him in *Time* had been, it did him no justice at all in person.

This flesh and blood version was virile, charismatic, sexy as hell. This close, she could see the myriad expressions in his eyes as he looked at her. And the main expression made her clit throb.

"I don't believe in playing coy games. And you're not like the rest of the guests."

"You're very sure of yourself, aren't you?"

"I know what I want. And I always get it."

"Or everything you've just said you weren't going to say could just be one huge, cocky line carefully designed to get you the same result."

His jaw tightened a touch but his avid stare continued to bore into her. To hypnotize her. "It's not a line, Bethany. You know that. You've just admitted you felt it. What I felt when I saw you from this room—you felt it, too, even before we'd exchanged a single word."

Although she wanted to agree, Bethany held back. Her instincts screamed that giving in too easily to this man would be dangerous. "It's a long cake walk from feelings to fucking, Mr. Savage." Even his surname tasted foreign on her tongue, exotic and exciting, and charged with the endless possibilities shimmering in his eyes.

His nostrils flared. "Not for us. In our minds, we've already fucked a hundred times in a hundred different ways. Mental copulation is just as powerful as the real thing."

Jesus! "And did I like it, this hypothetical fucking?"

He grinned with complete and utter masculine confidence, his white-toothed smile transfixing her. "You wouldn't be here, alone with me, if you hadn't."

"Mr. Savage—"

"Zach," he insisted.

"Let's be clear on one thing. I'm not in the habit of jumping into bed with the first man who crooks his finger at me on a Sunday morning."

His nostrils flared in a barely contained hint of displeasure. "You won't be jumping into bed with any other man for the foreseeable future. Let's get that clear."

The breath she blew out was both desperate and exasperated. His closeness was doing things to her insides she wasn't sure she could accurately describe. From the moment she'd set eyes on him, her nipples had peaked into tight, hard nubs.

Bethany was sure there was some sort of physical side effect from being this turned on for too long. The racing of her heart alone scared the holy shit out of her. She needed to get out of here, if only to find a moment's reprieve. But from staring into his eyes, she knew Zachary Savage wasn't about to let her go.

"Are you going to conduct this search sometime today, or am I free to go board your plane?"

For an eternity he didn't reply. Then he took a single step back. "Drop your purse."

Holding his gaze, she did as he asked without argument. With a soft thud, her purse landed on the carpet beside them. Until she didn't have the imagined security of her purse, she hadn't realized just how vulnerable she felt.

She swallowed hard and waited.

"Arms up."

A shiver went through her, but she complied, slowly lifting her arms until they were level with her shoulders.

"Higher," he rasped, his voice strangely compelling.

Licking her dry lips, she raised her arms higher until they were above her head. The action lifted her short dress.

Bethany didn't have to look down to know her legs were exposed to mid-thigh, that her breasts were pushed high by her stance.

She watched him watch her, her breath coming in pants as he slowly sank down onto his heels.

He reached for the heel of her shoe, lifted her foot and widened her stance. Then he grasped her foot and placed it on his knee. Her platform-heeled shoe came off with little resistance.

The moment Zachary Savage touched her, Bethany knew she was thoroughly screwed.

Profound, electric and wild. She marveled that so simple a touch on her heel could elicit such strong feelings.

With precise movements, he looked into her shoe, checked the platform and stiletto, then set it aside. He conducted the same scrutiny on her other shoe, then lowered her foot.

He raised his head and locked his dark grey eyes on her as his fingers drifted up her ankles and over her calves. When he touched the back of her knees, she couldn't stop a soft moan from escaping her throat. He paused, his stare curious and hungry, then he continued upward, upward until his hands were underneath her dress, over the super-sensitive skin of her hips.

Searching fingers grazed the edge of her panties, traced the cotton to the space between her legs. Bethany saw him swallow as his fingers encountered her wet heat. But he didn't linger.

Lips clamped together as if holding himself together with the utmost control, he let his fingers drift to the top edge of her panties and then to the sides before withdrawing.

She almost groaned in disappointment as he continued his search over her dress. Large, strong hands travelled around her waist, his grip sure and powerful as he searched upward over her midriff.

He rose to tower over her. Without her heels, she reached just below his shoulders. Again, her feeling of vulnerability escalated. He was so tall, so strong and powerful. He could break her with a single snap.

And yet, looking into his face, she saw gentleness in the depths of all that wild and savage need.

Zachary Savage wouldn't hurt her.

But if he chose to just rest his hands beneath her breasts like that, he could certainly kill her with lust.

As if sensing her agitation, he moved his fingers, followed

the line of her bra without palming her breast the way she yearned for him to.

Although... Sweet Jesus. This was sexier than she'd ever imagined. Way sexier. This push and play between them, the touching and yet not touching...

When his hands grasped her waist tightly and insistently before he let go, she bit her lip against another groan.

"Turn around."

Her sex pulsed harder, liquid heat pooling between her thighs. A hairsbreadth away from becoming one hot mess, she turned and placed heated hands against the cool glass.

This time he started from the top.

He lifted her hair and fingered the heavy tresses with long, slow movements.

At one point, Bethany thought he lifted a strand to his nose and inhaled, but her senses were so overwhelmed that she couldn't be sure.

Again, he searched the straps of her bra then moved lower to her waist.

He was just about to skim her panties when the click of the intercom echoed through the room.

"Would Indigo Lounge guests make their way to the VIP room, please? Boarding is about to commence."

She exhaled in a rush and started to lower her arms.

"Not yet. There's no rush."

"But we... I have to go."

He stepped closer and caged her in, one hand either side of her on the wall. "I own the plane, beautiful," he whispered in her ear. "It doesn't fly unless I say so."

"Okay, but you're offering a service and you have a duty to provide a great one."

"I also have a duty to make sure my rules are upheld. And

you're not leaving this room until I'm sure you're fully compliant with my wishes."

His fingers walked up the glass to rest over hers. Interlacing their fingers, he slowly lowered their arms. He let go of her hands and he shifted his stance behind her. His hands moved to her ass and another powerful surge of electricity scorched her. She closed her eyes against the potent sensation and whimpered like a helpless kitten.

He cupped the heavy globes, molded them, then squeezed tightly.

He muttered something she didn't quite catch, hard and urgent under his breath.

"What did you say?" she asked, her own breaths quick and frantic.

The intercom buzzed again, interrupting his reply and summoning guests to the VIP room.

Zach grunted his annoyance but when he spoke again, his voice held only dark, heated, implacable promise. This time when he caged her, he pushed right against her, until the hard, rigid imprint of his body was unmistakable against her back. He gripped her backside and pushed against her till his thick, heavy cock rested between her ass cheeks.

"Soon. Very soon, when the time is right, Bethany Green, I'm going to put my cock between these gorgeous peaches and I'm going to crack-fuck you until you beg me to make you come. And that will be just the beginning."

* * *

"Omigod, he said that? He actually said that?"

Bethany held the phone closer to her ear as she examined yet another bottle of eau de toilette in her spacious, jaw-droppingly stunning cabin. She'd run out of fingers to count the many luxuries spread all around her. Just as she'd run out of how many times she'd replayed that conversation in the office over and over in her mind.

"Which part, Keel?"

"The 'call me Zach and scream my name when I make you come' part, of course. Jeez!"

"Yep, he said that."

"And what did you say?"

Bethany paused and shifted the phone to her other ear. "I told him he couldn't call me Beth when I made him come because only one person calls me Beth, and I didn't think he'd want me thinking of my father when I was in a compromising position."

Keely erupted in laughter. "You didn't!"

"Nah, not really, but I may have thought it." Bethany breathed again. She didn't feel guilty for skimming over the office episode because she wasn't sure herself exactly what had happened. Also, that last statement of his felt too intimate, too raw to share. Who'd have thought the idea of being crack-fucked would turn her on so much!

She'd lost half of her mind the moment she'd laid eyes on Zachary Savage. The other half had gone the moment he'd put his hands on her.

As she relived those electrifying minutes in his office, heat engulfed her.

Walking beside him and the other guests onto the plane had been the hardest thing Bethany had done in recent memory.

For one thing, she'd been sure every single one of the twenty-four Indigo Lounge guests knew what she'd been up to in Zachary Savage's office. And also her panties had been so wet, every step had been a tortuous reminder of her scandalous behavior.

The last straw had been when Zachary had waved her before him at the foot of the jet steps.

"After you," he'd said in that sexy-as-hell voice.

She'd immediately shaken her head. "No, after you this time. I insist."

His knowing smile had made her face flame. But it hadn't stopped her from ogling his tight butt as he'd mounted the steps into the plane.

Once inside though, sexual chemistry had been replaced with another equally potent sensory bombardment.

The interior of the Airbus 380 was exquisite. White and gold with indigo trimmings, the space remodeled exclusively for high-net-worth clients was so stunning that Bethany forgot to breathe as she looked around.

A bar area, where mimosas and tiny croissants topped with shaved truffles were being handed out, stood to one side. Large, sumptuous club seats in groups of four were scattered up the mid-point of the plane. Beyond that, separated by a gold, white and indigo pearl-drop curtain, she spied another seating area.

She accepted a mimosa from a waitress—another stunner, although a redhead this time—and whirled slowly as her gaze lifted.

Above her, a Swarovski crystal chandelier twirled, throwing dazzling light over the group.

"Wow," she murmured.

"You like it?" Zach enquired from beside her.

She lowered her head and stared at him, feeling breathless all over again when she looked into his magnificent face. "Like it? I love it. It's stunning!"

He inclined his head but not before she saw a hint of pride

wash over his face. That single expression sent a pulse of something she couldn't quite define through her.

He was pleased by her praise. Bethany wasn't sure how it was possible that she'd met him less than an hour ago, yet already she felt as if she knew him on some visceral level. The knowledge that her opinion meant something to him touched her deep inside.

"I'm glad," he murmured.

"Why?" she asked, curiosity about him making her bold. "Why are you glad?"

"Because I want your trip to be memorable. Unforgettable. I will not achieve that if you're unhappy with your surroundings. If there's anything you need, just say the word and it'll be yours."

"Well, you needn't worry on that score. This is unbelievable."

His smile showed genuine pleasure. She gaped at the transformation from gorgeous to incredible, an undefinable feeling shooting through her.

"Thank you." He took a sip of his mimosa, his eyes fixed on her. "I'll give you a tour after takeoff."

"Don't I have a personal guide for that?"

"Why make do with an employee when you can have the boss man?"

"Maybe I don't want the boss man. Maybe I find the boss man a little overwhelming," she countered.

He grinned, his face once more transforming from intensely breathtaking to stop-your-heart charming.

In that moment, Bethany realized she wanted to see more of that smile. Not that the intense brooding looks didn't have their benefits. It was just that she feared for her cardiac functionality if he kept up with that electrifying intensity.

"I'll go slow, I promise."

Somehow the husky entreaty didn't allay her fears. But she found herself nodding all the same.

"Soooo? Have you had the tour yet?" Keely's question pierced her thoughts.

As Bethany refocused, a small shiver went through her. "No. He's coming to get me in five minutes." A quick glance in the bathroom mirror showed the excitement in her eyes. Whirling, she made her way back into her small living room, all the while willing her pulse to slow.

It was just a tour of the plane, a part of the normal Indigo Lounge service. Nothing else.

Yeah, right.

"Remember I need photographic evidence."

"I don't think I'm allowed to take pictures of the plane's interior."

"Not of the plane, dummy. Of Mr. Sexy-And-Reclusive."

"Oh." Bethany frowned. "I can't just take a picture of him, Keel."

"Of course you can. You just have to wait until he's passed out from you fucking his brains out."

Bethany laughed then jumped when she heard the knock on her door.

"He's here. I have to go," she whispered, then cringed at the breathlessness in her voice.

"Go. Have fun. Don't spend one second thinking of your sex-deprived friend."

Bethany stopped with her hand on the door. "Right. Remind me again which of us has had more sex in the last month than the other's had in the last year?"

Keely's smug laugh rang in her ears. "Guilty!"

"If I didn't love you so much, I'd want to kill you." She blew a kiss down the line, hung up and opened her door.

Zach Savage leaned against the doorjamb, looking dangerously gorgeous. His angled body made the material of his T-shirt stretch sensuously over a sculpted chest and ripped stomach. Following the grooves and landscape of his body made her mouth dry.

Before she slipped from merely observing to downright ogling, she forced her gaze upward, then bit back a gasp when she met his stunning eyes again.

He quirked a brow, grey eyes scrutinizing her from head to toe before trapping her gaze. With that one single look, he made her whole body tingle wildly.

"Ready?" he asked.

Bethany was certain he was asking about more than just the tour.

Was she ready for whatever was in store for her?

You need to move on. Forget Chris-A-Hole and his newfound love of anal of the male variety.

She sucked in a breath, both to sooth the pain in her heart and to gird her loins.

When she nodded, Zach straightened and held out a hand. A feeling of inevitability washed over her as she stepped next to him and placed her hand in his.

4

"So, who's had more sex in the last month than you've had in the last year?"

He dropped the question so casually that she stumbled halfway up the stairs to the upper deck.

Zachary caught her arm just below the elbow and steadied her. As if she didn't have enough to contend with, now she looked like a klutz. Which in turn annoyed her.

She faced him on the stairs, another shock exploding in her belly when her eyes clashed with his. "You were eavesdropping?"

"I was waiting for you to answer your door. You chose to speak within my earshot," he answered without a hint of remorse as his eyes did that raking-over-her-face thing she found hot and unnerving.

"Even if that's what happened, don't you think it's a bit inappropriate to repeat a private conversation?"

His lips firmed as he rested his hand a single inch from hers on the railing. "Maybe, but I can't un-hear what I heard, Bethany. And I told you, I'm not good at pretending. So I can't pretend I'm not interested in who you were talking to. Especially not when you were discussing a subject matter that holds a certain importance to me."

Her heart hammered at the strangely hypnotizing effect of his words. She fought very hard to think rationally. This was the real world, albeit a rarefied one right now—but the real world nevertheless. People didn't say things like that to each other.

"How can it hold importance to you? We met a little over two hours ago."

He regarded her as if he could see right through her, to the heart of her every need. Her every desire.

"Answer the question, Bethany," he said simply.

"I was talking to a friend." She moved away from him then whirled back to face him, irritated by the compulsion to answer and also by his demand to know intimate details about her. "Let's get something straight right now. What happened in your office doesn't give you the right to probe into my private conversations."

His hands fisted at his sides, and she once again got the impression that he was stopping himself from reaching for her. "I beg to differ, but if you prefer we can take this slower—"

"Or we can stop whatever this is dead in its tracks," she said. Bethany wasn't afraid to admit that the direction of the conversation disturbed her. There was a look in his eyes, one that implied a possessiveness that thrilled and bothered her at the same time. No man had ever looked at her with the focus and intensity with which Zachary Savage did. It made her palms damp and her heart race as if she'd run a marathon. She passed her tongue over her lower lip and, when he zeroed in on that telling movement, sucked in a breath. "Umm, maybe this tour was a bad idea. I can get my personal guide to—"

A single shake of his head, and a long black curl fell between his eyes. With a casual hand, he raked it back.

"No, we'll shelve this discussion for later. I promised you a tour. I think you'll find this upper deck even more interesting than the lower deck." He smiled, but the smile didn't quite reach his eyes. He fell into step beside her and went through a wide arch.

Her eyes widened as she took in the vista before her. On the far side, a stage had been set up, clearly for music entertainment.

"We have a rock band, Friday's Child, on board. They'll be providing the music for the Shanghai and Aleutian Islands trips. But there are other forms of entertainment on board, too. We pick up a new crew every two cities to give the guests a fresh experience and to allow the crew a break."

She looked over to the opposite side of the area. Intimate seating provided private entertainment areas, and even across the vast space, she saw a pole that only had one purpose. "Are the pole dancers specially invited or can anyone join in and have a turn?"

"All entertainment is provided by The Indigo Lounge, but guests are at liberty to participate as much or as little as they wish. The objective is to have a great time away from unwanted scrutiny."

"Right, I see."

Within another space, a private screening area had been set up, although the booths were unlike anything she'd seen in a regular cinema. They were high and extremely sequestered with indigo-colored velvet screens to ensure utmost privacy. Each seating area could accommodate a group of ten. A tallboy drawer was carved into the end of each row of seats. She pulled open the first of the five drawers and her eyes widened.

Sex toys in all shapes and sizes, including an exact replica of what she carried in her own luggage, graced the top drawer. The second contained bull whips and handcuffs in varying sizes.

Slowly, she slid the drawers shut and glanced up to find Zach's eyes on her.

"I take it you don't show just cartoons here?" A blush rushed to her face as their eyes clashed.

Again, that smile that barely touched his lips. "No, but if you crave cartoons, I'm sure I can find you something from our extensive selection."

He led her through another coded door. Delicate Oriental music chimed through inconspicuous speakers. When her eyes acclimatized to the low lighting, she saw massage beds grouped in intimate pairs and surrounded by fat, unlit candles. A hostess, dressed in a short indigo tank dress with gold piping, appeared from behind a discreet curtain and bowed.

"Our masseuses offer a whole range of therapies," Zachary explained in a low voice. "All you need to do is ask and it'll be done. Travelling, even in the lap of luxury, can be quite exhausting," he murmured. "What better way to relax than with a massage, either individually or with someone special?" His voice reeked pure sex.

On the one hand, Bethany was relieved that his frosty anger had receded, but he was back to his sexily lethal self, and as she glanced at him and saw his narrow-eyed gaze on her, she knew relief was the last thing she should be feeling.

The last space he showed her blew her clean away. They stood at the nearest point to the nose of the plane where a panoramic window revealed a clear one-hundred-and-eighty-degree view. Since they were only an hour into their trip and clear of the clouds below, all Bethany could see was pure blue sky. She leaned against the railing in front of her and stretched up on her toes to get a better look.

"Wow," she breathed.

He leaned in behind her, his hands on either side of hers on the railing. He caged her in, just as he'd done in his office, and her breath stalled in her throat as he moved in close.

"I'll bring you up here in a few hours just before the sun goes down," he said in a low voice, which pulsed with dark, sultry promise even when he wasn't saying anything sexual. "It's incredible to see the twilight sky as the stars come out."

She'd heard Keely go ape-shit over some actor's voice, but Bethany had never experienced sexual arousal for that reason. Until now. She felt a low drag in her stomach and wished he would keep speaking so she could melt in his voice.

"I'd... I'd really like that."

"Good." They stayed like that for several minutes, watching the view in warm silence as the jet raced east. With her every breath, she became more and more caught up in his scent, in the essence of Zach Savage and the incredible things his aura did to her.

"I didn't mean to pry into your life earlier." He stopped and she felt him shake his head. "No, scratch that. I meant to do exactly that."

"Why?" she asked.

"Because I want to know every single detail about you, Bethany. I won't apologize if that seems excessive or forward; it's the truth."

Her breath caught and her grip on the railing tightened. She felt as if she were swaying even though she didn't move. "You really don't believe in sugar-coating your words, do you?"

"There's no room for ambivalence in my life. I'm required to make huge decisions every day. I can't afford to mince my words."

"But surely that applies in your business life, not your private one?" she asked, still unable to move from where he'd imprisoned her.

He moved closer still, until his pelvis brushed against her ass. Heat flushed through her. She looked down at their hands, her delicate ones next to his strong and powerful grip. So close and yet not touching.

"When it comes right down to it, the same principles apply in all areas of my life. I won't mislead you into thinking this is something more or less than it is or will ever be. I want you. I intend to have you and I'll do whatever it takes to achieve that goal, including finding out everything I can about you. You can help by answering my questions."

"You know, you could simply say that you'd like to get to know me, and let this thing evolve more naturally."

His small exhalation of breath told her he was chuckling. She kept her gaze focused forward. They might have met only a short time ago, but she already knew a smiling Zachary Savage was lethal to her senses.

"Indeed. And it was what I intended to do at the end of the tour. But then the subject of sex came up. I haven't been able to think of anything else since."

"I guess I understand how that could derail the best intentions."

He laughed, a low, rich, gorgeous sound that shot heat straight to her core. His fingers gripped the railing tighter, then he eased his hands closer to hers.

But still he didn't touch her. There was something about the delayed gratification of that move that made her insides clench.

"So, have dinner with me tonight."

Before she could respond, she heard voices as a group entered the sky-viewing area.

Zachary stiffened and she heard his low growl just before he stepped away.

Sucking in a long-denied full breath, she turned, careful to keep her hold on the railing because of her decidedly shaky legs.

The first group included a sultan or sheikh of some sort if the attire he wore was a guess. He was accompanied by four women ranging from early to mid-twenties. Each woman was dressed in stunning designer gear with priceless jewelry and impeccable make up. And they all pandered to him as if they worshipped the ground he walked on.

"He's the son of a sultan. Those are his wives," Zach murmured as the women caught their first glimpse of the sky and giggled excitedly.

Bethany barely stopped her face from contorting into a grimace. "Right, because why have one wife when four will do?"

Striking grey eyes latched onto hers, deadly serious in their intensity. "Rest assured, I'm a one-woman man, Bethany. As long as I have your word that you're a one-man woman, we won't have a problem. Because I will devote my every waking moment to ensuring your pleasure so you don't have to look elsewhere for it. Do I have your word?"

"I—"

Sultan Junior saw Zachary and threw his arms out with a loud and effusive greeting. Zachary emitted another frustrated growl. He threw her an apologetic glance.

"Excuse me. I was hoping to stay under the radar, but I guess that's blown out of the water now."

She waved him off, unable to keep from watching his sexy swagger as he walked away.

Dear God. On the one hand, she knew what was happening. The calm before the storm; the foreplay before the fucking. But if anyone had warned Bethany she would be this turned on by it, she'd have laughed herself hoarse.

At twenty-four, she'd had far fewer sex partners than the

average woman her age, her longest relationship being with her fourth boyfriend, Chris—until his bombshell announcement six months ago.

She'd moved to New York because of him, had moved in with him at his request, and for the best part of a year, she'd fooled herself into thinking they were in the final stages of courtship before the big proposal. At first, the weekend business trips hadn't tweaked her radar. But after eight weekends in a row and the disconcerting knowledge that she was having more sex with Dildo Pete than with Chris, she'd known something was seriously wrong.

But not even in her wildest raging nightmares had she dreamed the man she'd thought she'd spend the rest of her life with would confess he now preferred men.

"Hey, there."

She dragged herself from Fucked Up Memory Lane to find the guy she'd seen at the check-out desk in front of her. The rest of his group had also arrived on the deck with their hostess and were checking out the view.

"Uh... hi." She hoped her smile didn't reveal her inner thoughts.

He held out a hand. "I'm Jackson Blaine. Friends call me Jax."

"Bethany," she replied, and shook his hand. His face was open and friendly, with sparkling brown eyes and a dimpled smile that set her at ease. All in all, he was very easy on the eyes.

"I'm a drummer with Friday's Child. We're gigging in a couple of hours on the lower deck. Stop by if you want."

She was about to nod when she glanced past him and felt the force of Zachary Savage's narrow-eyed stare. A shiver coursed through her, and her heart skipped several beats before it attempted to right itself.

"I... I'll think about it."

"Great." Jax smiled. "That's some view, huh?" He indicated the sky beyond the deck.

With monumental effort, she tore her gaze from Zach, but not before she saw his attention swing to Jax.

"Yes, it's incredible." She turned and stared unseeingly at the view, another shiver coursing through her. She didn't need to look at him to know she was still the subject of Zachary Savage's focus.

Beside her, Jax talked a bit. She made appropriate answers until his group joined him. Introductions were made that she barely remembered.

She managed to nod when he smiled.

"So, see you in a couple of hours?"

"Why will you be seeing him in a couple of hours?"

Zach had materialized beside her. Again he stood close, so very close, but didn't touch her. She wondered whether he'd practiced that particular move, or whether it came naturally to him, an inherent part of his sexual aura. Whatever it was, it turned her on so damned fiercely that she wanted to growl. She, who'd never once growled in her life.

"Friday's Child just invited me to a gig."

His brows clamped with displeasure. "I changed my plans because of you. Mingling with the other guests doesn't interest me."

Again, his arrogance irritated her. But the knowledge that he'd changed his plans because of her turned her on—much more than she could rationally cope with.

Jesus, she needed to claw back some reason here, before she lost her damned mind.

"But it interests me. I promised Keely I'd try and leave my suite at least once a day."

He stiffened and leaned closer. "Who's Keely?"

"Someone I care about."

"And why is having fun important to you on this trip?"

"Because..." She stopped and wondered again why she felt the need to bare all to this man. The easiest thing would've been to tell him to mind his own business and leave her alone.

But she didn't want Zachary Savage to leave her alone. In fact, it was the very last thing she wanted him to do. "Because I need to put some ghosts to rest."

His eyes gleamed, went a little hard, then settled back into their usual intense focus. He nodded and again his gaze dropped to her mouth. "I know a little bit about ghosts, sweetheart. Let me help."

"I hardly know you."

"I can help with that too. Leave your suite. Move into mine."

5

He was serious. Of course he was. One thing she was learning very quickly about Zachary Savage was that he didn't say things he didn't mean. The shiver that went through her shook her to the depths of her soul.

"My suite is perfectly adequate, but thank you for the offer."

"I'm not inviting you to my bed, Bethany. Not yet."

Disappointment shot through her, but Keely had taught her a passable poker face, which she prayed would stick now. "Pray tell, why not?"

"The time isn't right."

"Hypothetically speaking, if I won't be sharing your bed, then why invite me at all...? Right, it's a possessive thing."

The group had started to leave the sky-viewing area. When she started to follow, he restrained her. "I don't think I need to keep an eye on you"—he ignored her shocked snort and continued—"I just want to reassure myself that your needs are met until the appropriate time when we can take this to the next level. Besides, this is technically my place of work, and I don't fuck where I work, although I'm seriously tempted to make an exception for you."

"You seriously expect me to believe you've never had sex on your plane before?"

His eyes darkened, became inscrutable. "Not on my Indigo planes, no."

"But you're a member of the mile high club?"

He paused for several seconds. "A tacky term, I find, but yes, I've had sex on a plane. If you desire a similar experience, I'll provide you with one, but it won't be on this plane."

She grew hot and bothered. The look in his eyes promised all sorts of filthy sin. Her nipples puckered, strained against her dress. His gaze dropped to her breasts. A slow smile curved his lips when he witnessed the evidence of his words on her.

"Does that turn you on, Bethany? The thought of being fucked on a plane as we race toward the stars?"

"I plead the fifth."

His smile widened. "I get the feeling you won't be a walk in the park."

"I told you, it's a long cake walk between—"

"Feelings and fucking, yes, I remember. Which is why I want you to have dinner with me. I want to work on shortening the walk."

"If dinner is a euphemism for talking me into moving into your suite, the answer is no."

"It involves a lot more, but I accept your answer to this particular question."

Surprise rocked her. "You do?"

He nodded. "It was a desperate Hail Mary, which, I admit, would've been more problematic in the long run. No need to torture us both until we get off this plane." His gaze refocused on her lips and stayed there. Then he breathed in slowly as if reinforcing his willpower.

Bethany licked her lips as several chaotic emotions rushed through her.

"Say yes, Bethany. It's just dinner and conversation."

They both knew it was a lot more, but she went along with the ruse.

"Jeez, I don't know—a boring dinner or an evening with a rock band."

His smile was self-assurance personified. "Dinner with me won't be boring. I guarantee you that."

She believed him, although she didn't give him the satisfaction of saying that. A man with his charisma could read the dictionary backwards and make it sound sexy. "Be that as it may, I make my own decisions. And I didn't quite hear you ask me to dinner. I don't respond well to demands."

"Come anyway, I have a proposition for you."

"We only just met. How could you possibly have a proposition for me?"

He sobered and regarded her with a look that held a hint of reproach. "We can do a merry dance around this if you want, Peaches. But all we're doing is wasting time." His gaze hardened. "Unless you're not free to be with me?"

"If I wasn't, do you think I'd come on a trip like this on my own?"

He swallowed, a look of sheer relief on his face that sent a pulse of emotion through her. Why had she thought him enigmatic when she'd first seen him and read about him? Zach Savage wore his emotions on his sleeve.

No, that wasn't quite correct. There were some emotions he wasn't afraid to exhibit. She'd seen the way he behaved with his employees and with the guests on the plane. To them, he wore a smile that said "friendly, but keep away." And yet with her, so far he'd displayed displeasure, annoyance, pride and an ever-present, all-encompassing hunger.

"Then there's nothing to stop you."

"No, there's nothing. Except me."

"You'd stop yourself from enjoying my company just for the sake of proving to me that you can?"

She shrugged. "I may not want to. Don't think you know me just because our bodies react a certain way to one another, Zachary."

His eyes darkened. "I love the way you say my name. I might let you call me Zachary after all."

"Why, thank you for the honor."

Her snarky tone caught his attention. He sighed. "Bethany, what's this about? All I want is your company."

"No, I seriously doubt that."

"You're right, I want a whole lot more. But for now I just want dinner."

She sighed. "Okay. Just dinner. Your place at eight?"

He inclined his head in a way that made him look almost regal. "I'll come and collect you."

"No. Philip, my very able bodyguard who I met so very briefly before you commandeered my attention, will escort me."

His eyes gleamed a hint of displeasure, but he nodded. "I'm going to enjoy making you turn all these nos into yeses."

She summoned a smile from somewhere, despite the fact that looking into those eyes of his made her head spin. "Good luck with that."

He stepped closer, lowered his head as if to kiss her.

Bethany's lungs seized, her whole body poised for the contact, but at the last moment, he froze and stepped back.

In silence, he escorted her back to her suite. She passed

Tracy, her hostess, who smiled at them, but Bethany read the questions in her wide-eyed look.

At her door, he leaned against the doorjamb as she entered her code. "Right, see you later," she said as the door clicked open.

He straightened then slowly brushed his fingers over her cheek, a caress that stroked every single nerve in her body. Against her better judgment, she started to sway toward him. But again, he froze and jammed his hands into his back pockets the way he had before. "See you at eight. Don't be late."

"I'm never late," she threw back.

His husky laugh as he walked away resonated through her for a very long time.

* * *

For dinner, she chose a mid-thigh, black leather China-doll dress coupled with black patterned tights and platform pumps.

Catching her hair up in a loose knot, she completed the look with silver chandelier earrings and her favorite scarlet lipstick.

Philip, a burly, towering giant of a man from Papua New Guinea, knocked on her door at five to eight sharp.

He returned her smile with a bow. "Good evening, Miss Green." He stepped back and waited until she'd shut her door.

To her surprise, he led her toward the back of the plane to a hitherto unseen private elevator.

"This will take you straight to Mr. Savage's suite. Enjoy your evening."

She maintained her poker smile until the elevator doors shut, then she breathed out and glanced around at the chrome and jet-polished interior. Even the small space screamed unimaginable wealth.

When it opened several seconds later, Zachary Savage stood in the doorway, dressed in a white shirt and black slacks, which hugged lean hips and powerful thighs and did unspeakable things to her system.

To take her mind off it, she blurted, "You have your own elevator?"

One brow quirked, as did his smile. "I have my own everything, Bethany. You'll soon discover that I'm a man who intensely dislikes sharing."

He stood to one side and ushered her inside.

His suite was smaller than hers, which surprised her. But the space was nevertheless as divine as the rest of the plane.

He poured a glass of Chianti and passed it to her. Then he settled his tall, mouthwatering frame next to her on the sofa.

The moment he turned his attention on her, her breath caught in her lungs.

Jesus, everything this guy did was lethal, including just sitting and staring.

"Dinner will be served in a few minutes. That gives me just enough time to put my proposition to you."

Bethany sipped her wine to buy herself more time. Because everything inside her was poised to scream yes to whatever he said. Which scared the living shit out of her.

"I'm listening."

"I want to be your guide in Shanghai. We'll condense the two days into one day, but I'll make sure you see all the important sights. Then I want you to ditch the Indigo Lounge experience and come to Marrakech with me."

* * *

Zach watched her stunning face go through a myriad of expressions. He held his breath, forcing himself to remain still as his question ricocheted through her mind.

Jesus, he'd never wanted a woman as much as he wanted her. The fact that he couldn't have her immediately, that his integrity demanded he set things right elsewhere, ate at him like a damned disease.

That dress she was wearing, the leather that came up to mid-thigh—Christ, it was a miracle he could remain conscious while all his blood was rushing south. As for those ridiculous bow patterns on her tights, he would gladly have torn them to shreds with his teeth to get to her soft, endlessly arousing flesh.

Instead, he sipped his drink and waited for her to answer.

"What's in Marrakech?"

He exhaled in relief. It wasn't a definite yes... but she wasn't saying no. And he'd be damned if he was prepared to give her the chance to say no.

"One of my homes. It's at the foothills of the Atlas Mountains with the desert oasis right at your fingertips."

She jerked and her eyes went wide. "An oasis as in, there's a body of water there?" she whispered, her face growing a little pale.

Zach frowned, hating the expression in her eyes. "You don't like the water?"

She pursed bee-stung lips—lips he was dying to kiss—and shook her head. "I'm not a big fan of any body of water."

Shit. That could be a problem. But not one he intended to let stand in the way of his goals. Because having Bethany Green had become his number one mission. She drew him like a moth to a flame. He wanted to burn in her heat, die in her fire.

He had no idea what was happening, what had started happening when he'd first laid eyes on her, but hell if he was going to slow down to find out. He was well and truly captivated. The episode in his office had nearly blown his mind clean away. He'd never done anything like that before. In some circumstances, it could be grounds for some serious questions about his work practices, but at the time he hadn't given a damn. Hell, he'd do it again in a heartbeat.

Seeing her and claiming her had been a natural progression that he hadn't questioned for a single moment. He intended that progression to advance all the way to his bedroom.

"There will be other things to explore besides the water. Many, many other things."

At his blatant answer, a flush heated her cheeks. Exquisite blue eyes, set within an even more exquisite face, stared at him. She took another sip of wine and licked a drop off her lower lip.

His low groan made her eyes widen even further.

"How long do we have to stay in Shanghai?"

"The I.L. stops there for two days. We can do a twelve-hour abbreviated tour."

"So Marrakech means I'll miss the rest of the tour?"

"Yes."

Her plump lower lip pouted. "I was quite looking forward to Bora Bora."

"I will give you Bora Bora. I have a place there too. But before we do that, I have business to take care of in Paris, then in Morocco. Then I'm free to be with you. I don't want to leave you. Say yes, Bethany."

She sucked in a breath. One that pressed her generous breasts against the leather and displayed her tight, hard nipples. When she uncrossed her long legs and re-crossed them, Zach felt the pulse hammer at his temples. He wanted those legs splayed wide for him as he tongued her plump clit and watched her come, over and over. Then he wanted them high around his shoulders as he drove his cock into her.

His dick hardened so fast and painfully that he nearly grabbed it to ease the intense discomfort.

As if sensing his agitation, her gaze locked on his then dropped to his crotch. She couldn't miss her effect on him, and he didn't bother to hide it. He wanted her to see how hot he was for her. How much he desired her.

Slowly, she licked her lips. Her breath came out in soft, hot pants. Then her lids lifted and she murmured the word he wanted to hear.

"Yes."

6

Shanghai was hot, humid and glorious.

Her emperor suite at the Indigo Mandarin Shanghai—she'd discovered that all the Indigo Lounge destinations were linked to businesses owned by Zachary Savage—had made her want to weep with joy, but it was the thought of being escorted round the amazing Chinese city that made Bethany's blood thrum with excitement.

Of course, her escort also had a lot to do with it.

A full twelve hours after the fact, she found it hard to believe she'd readily agreed to abandon the trip of a lifetime and said yes to Zach. A part of her remained suspended in disbelief at what she was contemplating. The rest of her felt compelled to seize the moment, give in to the incredible chemistry that sizzled between them every time he looked at her with those intense grey eyes.

She felt him behind her and turned from examining the enormous jade Buddha and ancient carvings on the walls of the Jing'an Temple, their fourth and final tour stop.

"Are you ready to leave?" he asked, his low, growly voice making her heart race that little bit faster.

His hands were once again shoved into the back of his jeans, a familiar stance she was beginning to recognize every time he came within touching distance.

The blue shirt he'd worn stretched over his wide chest, and from the open collar she glimpsed vibrant, golden-brown skin that made her whole body tingle.

"Yes." Her voice emerged strained, and she shoved down the spurt of irritation that rose out of nowhere.

For some reason, Zachary Savage, having made it very plain that he wanted to get into her panties in the very near future, was going out of his way not to touch her. She knew it wasn't because he wanted to maintain a sense of propriety in front of his employees. For parts of their tour, he'd instructed Tracy, her personal guide, and Philip, her bodyguard, to give them privacy as he'd shown her around the exquisite Yuyuan Gardens.

But even when they were alone, although he stayed close, he was very careful not to touch her. The urge to ask him why hovered on the tip of her tongue, but she swallowed it down and curbed her own desire to step closer, slide her hands over that ripped, mouthwatering chest.

"Are you okay?"

She looked up and found him staring at her, eyes narrowed and probing in a way that made her fear he could read her thoughts.

Quickly, she nodded. "I'm fine, just a little worn out from trekking all over the city."

The boots she'd worn with her jeans and white lacy top were beginning to pinch hard, and her feet ached from the pace he'd set since they left the hotel at nine that morning, but her senses were on fire with the whole experience.

"You should've told me to slow down."

"What, and miss all the amazing places you've taken me today?"

He merely smiled, a devastating smile that sent heat through her stomach and made her clit pulsate.

"I'm glad you enjoyed it." He stepped back and indicated the limo idling on the curb outside the steps to the temple.

They drove through Pudong District and entered the heartland of cosmopolitan Shanghai, with skyscrapers and iconic towers that stretched into the sky.

"Thank you for showing me around," she said as the car drove them back to the hotel.

Bethany tried not to devour him with her eyes as he lounged next to her in the back seat. Of course, he had no such compunction. Every time she moved, his gaze followed. He tracked her with the focus of a jungle predator, and even though his stance remained graceful and relaxed, there remained a coiled energy about him that her hyperaware senses couldn't ignore.

"My pleasure," he said simply. One arm slid over the back of the seat, within a whisper of where the messy bun of her hair touched the headrest. Perhaps he even caught a strand between his fingers. She was much too overwhelmed with what his proximity did to her to find out.

Silence thrummed between them. One he didn't feel inclined to break. No, Zachary was content to just lounge like a predator in the sun and watch her. And she... she was getting worked up over the whole staring-but-not-touching crap going on. She turned her head as the Nanpu River came into view, but it didn't alleviate the awareness crawling over her skin.

She turned back to him. "So how many languages do you speak, besides Mandarin and English?"

"Five. Seven if you count slightly less salubrious words in two other languages," he replied.

"You mean swear words?"

His mouth curved in one of those wicked smiles. Her sex clenched hard and her nipples tightened into needy points.

"No, I mean fuck words, Bethany. I'm fluent in Greek and Armenian. If you like, I can describe your every move, your every sound and how your sweet cunt feels around my cock when we fuck. Do you like dirty talk during sex, Bethany?"

Fire engulfed her. Her hands clenched in her lap as she watched him lean closer, his gaze running feverishly over her face.

"Why is that important?" she managed to squeeze out.

"I want you to educate me in what pleases you; what turns you on. Just as I intend to teach you how to satisfy me." He leaned even closer, brought that heady smell of potent masculinity and expensive, exclusive aftershave with him.

Her senses reeled, as they'd been reeling since she walked into the private hangar yesterday.

"You want to know what pleases me?"

He nodded once.

"Finding out a little bit about the man I'm intending to abandon my trip for would be nice."

His gaze cooled and he relaxed back in his seat. Turning that mesmerizing gaze from her, he glanced out the window.

"You know who I am in all the ways that count."

"I beg to differ. I know your name and some of the businesses you're involved in. How do I know underneath those expensive clothes you're not really a seventy-year-old man addicted to plastic surgery and steroids?"

He laughed, a warm, rough sound that curled her toes.

"The plastic surgery is easy to prove. As is the steroid allegation."

More heat flooded her. She'd seen him aroused last night in his suite. His hard-on had been unmistakable beneath the soft material of his slacks. The size of it had made her throat dry and her sex tighten hungrily. No long-term steroid use there.

"Be that as it may. I need a little bit more. If it helps, I'll go first. I'm twenty-four, I turn twenty-five in two weeks. I moved to New York two years ago. Before that I lived at home in Westchester with my parents—both university professors—and I graduated summa cum laude from Cornell."

The smile he gave her was cryptic. "I know all of that."

Bethany felt a jolt of shock. "You do?"

He nodded. "Half of the information was in the forms you filled out."

"And the other half?"

His lips pursed for a split second. "Every Indigo Lounge guest is vetted thoroughly before they're approved for the experience. I was reading your papers when you arrived."

Her shock faded and she nodded. "That makes sense. So you know everything about me—"

"Not quite everything, but I intend to find out." The dark promise sent a mingled pulse of alarm and excitement through her.

"Will you afford me the same courtesy, then?"

He shrugged. "You know my name. I'm thirty-one. I'm heterosexual and I own several businesses across the globe. I like airplanes and baseball but don't get to watch or attend many games." His gaze re-fixed on her, that intensity claiming her with its forcefulness, then dropped to linger on her breasts before coming back to her face. "And right now, I can't think beyond the moment I get to fuck you."

He was giving her the glossy exterior, the fluff piece that anyone with internet access could find, then burying his reluctance to reveal anything about himself with talk of sex. She fought against the desire that dragged through her belly and tried to focus.

"What about family? Do you have any?"

An icy chill froze his face and darkened his eyes. She watched, stunned as his jaw clenched tight, and the man who'd been gazing hungrily at her a moment before completely disappeared.

"None that I want to talk about."

* * *

As definitive answers went, it was as stark and as blunt as it could get.

His arm dropped from the back of the bench seat, his hands curling into fists on his thighs as he turned to stare out the window.

Bethany watched his profile, struck anew by the sheer gorgeousness of Zachary Savage. Even with an icy scowl stamped across his face, the man was beyond-description-hot.

It was clear she'd broached a sensitive subject. She wanted to take back the question, but she bit her tongue.

Getting to know the man you intended to sleep with wasn't a crime. Hell, in this day and age of creeps at every corner, it was mandatory.

All the same, she held her breath when he sighed and turned to her.

"You probably have a few boxes you're dying to tick before you're reassured that what's going to happen between us is okay. Trust me, Bethany, it couldn't be more right. Would you be more reassured if I told you I've never done anything like this before?"

"You mean pick up a woman from one of your planes and make plans to sleep with her?"

One corner of his mouth lifted, but his face remained deadly serious. "I haven't flown on an Indigo Lounge flight since the maiden flight six years ago. And I've certainly never acted on the spur-of-the-moment to go on one."

Again, she experienced a bolt of shock, then she remembered his instructions at the airport. "Your crew were surprised you were changing your plans," she murmured.

"That's because I only stopped in Newark to refuel my jet. They were nearly done when you arrived. Another half hour and I would've been gone."

He let that last piece of information linger, let them both absorb the serendipity of their meeting. When his eyes met hers again, the cold was gone. And the desire was back full force and pounding into her, relentless and unyielding.

And yet, dammit, he made no move to touch her. Or to come any closer.

It was almost as if Zachary Savage was intent on seducing her with his words alone.

And what a bang-up job he was doing. Bethany shifted as she felt her panties dampen from the hungry look in his eyes. The tingle between her legs had taken on full throbbing status, and her breasts felt so heavy and full that she wanted to clamp her palms over them, squeeze them to alleviate their aching.

"So you see, everything else is superfluous. What's important is you and me and our desire to explore what's between us."

She was saved from answering when the car rolled to a stop beneath the exquisite portico of Zachary's hotel. When the porter saw who was in the car, he jumped to attention and rushed to open her door.

By the time he emerged on the walkway beside her, Zach had assumed the casually distant persona he'd displayed in company all day long. He responded to several greetings as he led her through the marble-floored, mouth-droppingly designed foyer to the bank of private elevators that serviced her suite and his.

The hotel was decorated like the rest of Zach's businesses she'd seen online and in person so far, touches of exquisite style with the barest hint of indigo that announced its master's personal touch.

They entered the elevator and he immediately turned to her.

"Remember we leave for the airport in four hours," he said as the doors shut, cocooning them in its intimate space as they were rushed up to the eighteenth floor.

It'd just turned six. She'd taken Tracy's advice and stayed acclimatized to the crazy time zone when they landed.

Zachary's private jet was picking them up in Paris, but they were flying commercial from Shanghai. "That gives me enough time for a massage before dinner," she said.

He sucked in a quick breath then jammed his hands into his pockets. A quick glance showed his eyes had darkened to slate. She didn't know whether the idea of her getting a massage turned him on or displeased him, because his face remained as neutral as it had been since they'd exited the limo.

"The Indigo Flame serves the best lobster in Shanghai. I've reserved a table for eight."

"Great. Friday's Child are performing at the club next door at nine, so that'll be perfect." Jax had sent her another message when she'd failed to attend their rehearsal on the plane. To refuse twice would be rude.

Again, she saw Zachary's lips purse, and this time she knew he was displeased.

Too bad. He had no right to emote, subtly or otherwise, when they hadn't even gotten to first base yet. Or when he seemed determined to keep himself at a distance.

The past few months had taught her that she was clearly unable to read men but despite that, Zachary Savage had made it clear—graphically clear—what he intended to happen between them. His words had left her so hot, she was milliseconds away from jumping him.

Except he seemed to be in no hurry to follow through. Being made a complete fool of by Chris had left scars she was terrified would never heal. The last thing she needed was mixed signals from another man.

"I'll get your concierge to make sure your bags are packed and ready to go when we're done with the concert."

That he'd conceded so quickly soothed her somewhat. But not enough to stop her from saying briskly, "No need. It's already sorted."

He raised an eyebrow.

"Tracy was looking lost after I told her I wouldn't be needing her this morning and that I was leaving early. She offered to pack and I accepted." The pretty brunette who had been assigned to her had asked if she'd done anything wrong. Bethany's quick assurance had pacified her. Getting her to sort out the luggage she'd barely unpacked had pleased the younger woman.

The doors opened and they stepped out. There were only two suites on this floor. She fetched her keycard from her purse and stopped in front of the door on the right.

Dropping her bag on the delicate cream console table, she

turned to find Zach leaning against the doorjamb. His gaze scoured the room then returned to rest on her.

"So I'll see you in about an hour?"

He nodded but made no move to leave. The look in his eyes made her throat dry.

"Something on your mind?" she asked, noting how husky her voice had grown.

"This is the last time you get a massage from anyone but me, Bethany."

The possessive throb in his voice made her stomach clench. "Enough with the highly charged words, Zach. For a man who constantly screws me with his eyes, the fact that you haven't even bothered to kiss me makes me wonder if you're all talk."

He jerked upright so fast her breath caught. He took a step forward, then stopped, fists clenched against his thighs. Her senses screamed with the need for him to close the space between them. But he just clamped his gorgeous lips together and shoved a hand through his thick black hair.

Realizing he wasn't going to come any closer made the insane need to feel his mouth on hers grow stronger. She watched him force control back into his body.

"We met thirty-eight hours and forty-six minutes ago, Bethany Green. I intend to extract a kiss from those bee-stung lips of yours for every minute of that time—when the time is right. I will kiss you till you beg for mercy. Then I'll kiss you elsewhere, right between your legs. I intend to eat you for hours, until you beg for my cock. And then I will fuck you until you pass out from screaming my name. And if you think those are just words, that I don't intend to rock your fucking world, then I feel sorry for you. Because the reality will blow your goddamn mind."

Her mouth was still gaping open after he'd turned on his

heel and left. It was only the sound of his door slamming from across the hall that roused her from her stupor.

In a semi-daze, she stared around the room, unfocused and unsteady. She stumbled to the exquisite divan and collapsed into it.

Without a doubt, Zachary Savage had a way with words. And she was discovering her body had developed a unique and heady way of responding to those words. She looked down and cringed when she saw her nipples erect, aching and clearly visible through her top.

"God!" Disgusted with herself, she jumped up and headed for the suite's bedroom.

By the time the sweet, middle-aged masseuse appeared fifteen minutes later, she'd talked herself down from the raging, sex-depraved stranger she'd become and back to being the normal, sex-deprived woman she was used to.

* * *

He'd meant it when he said he had no interest in the band. In fact, Zach seemed discomfited to the point of edginess, and they were barely thirty minutes into Friday's Child's private concert.

"You don't like rock bands, is that it?" She had to lean in close to be heard over the sound of the lead singer's growly number; close enough to feel the heat of Zach's skin just above the collar of his shirt and smell the tangy scent of his aftershave.

In the semi-smoky club, she could see women, and some men, giving him the once over and stopping to look again. Not once did he return their gazes or show interest. His attention was focused solely, squarely on her in a way that made her feel as if she was plugged permanently into an electrical feed caused by his eyes alone.

He shook his head, and a strand of his hair brushed her face. A tremble went through her.

"I like rock bands just fine."

"But?" she probed, wanting him to throw her a bone. Despite him saying they didn't need the superfluous contraptions of the whole getting-to-know-one-another thing, she wanted to know something about the enigma that was Zachary Savage.

He made a sound that was halfway between a sigh and a huff. "Someone I once knew loved their music. Hearing them brings back memories."

She was so shocked he'd given her something personal that she didn't want to acknowledge just what it was he'd told her. And she felt the next question bubble up before she could stop it. "Someone. Care to elaborate?"

His eyes darkened. "Not particularly."

Again, stark and blunt. He didn't have to say the words for her to know she needed to back off.

This time, she heeded the advice. Pulling her gaze from his forceful stare, she glanced towards the stage where the song was reaching its conclusion.

Jax went through an elaborate series of drum riffs, ending in a deafening crescendo that made the room go wild.

As they accepted the rousing applause, he looked over to her, pointed a drumstick at her and winked.

Blushing, she smiled and waved.

"You're giving him the wrong signals. Stop," Zach said, his voice holding an edge she was beginning to recognize.

"Excuse me?"

"Don't let him think you're available, because you're not. And before you challenge me on that, think about the futility of it for a moment. Would you rather spend your last hours in Shanghai arguing with me or enjoying the band?"

"I excel at multi-tasking. I can do both."

"Instead of arguing, you can tell me what's wrong with your feet," he said.

"My feet?"

"You've been rubbing your arches against that table leg for the last ten minutes."

"They hurt more than I thought they would. The masseuse asked if I wanted them rubbed but I declined because I didn't want to be late for dinner."

She'd been eager to see him again. And he seemed to know it. The smile he gave her sent goosebumps over her flesh. His lids descended and he seemed to debate with himself for several seconds. Then his warm palm slid under her calf and lifted her leg into his lap.

He started behind her knee. Warm, pleasurable hands kneaded her tight muscles in a sure massage that sucked the breath right out of her lungs and made her blood pound hard in her ears. His eyes fixed on her face, he applied a subtle pressure all the way down her leg until he hit the prerequisite spot, right in the middle of her foot.

Bethany couldn't help the moan that escaped her throat. He heard it. Grey eyes darkened to almost black and his nostrils flared in reaction. He pressed his thumb over the sleek muscle again, hard enough to cause pleasure and pain. Her sex throbbed violently.

"Do you like that?"

She was too far gone to even think of being equivocal. "Yes."

Her simple answer made him smile. It was a smug smile, full of unrestrained satisfaction. She'd given the man what he wanted. A feeling of unexpected pleasure fizzed through her.

"See how easy that was?" He increased the pressure, confirming that this wasn't the first time he'd given a foot massage. A hot lance went through her. Stunned, she realized she was jealous.

"Don't gloat, Savage," she snapped, trying to dispel the feeling. "It's a turn off. You give a good foot massage. Big deal."

His smile was lethally erotic. "I give good everything."

"And now you're just boasting."

He stared at her for a long moment then he looked around, a brief look of restless impatience accompanying the movement. "Do we have to stay here?" he asked.

"I'll answer that after you've seen to my other foot."

He did, so effectively that the moan she'd sworn not to utter again leapt out before she could stop herself.

His grip tightened for a second. "God, I can't wait to hear you moan like that when I'm balls-deep inside you."

Her foot jerked at the image that rose in her mind. He pulled her foot closer, deeper into his crotch. When she realized just what the pad of her foot rested on, she gasped.

He was large and full and solid as steel. Before she could dismiss the thought, her foot flexed against him.

His groan was low and thick, a sound that rumbled along her nerves and struck straight between her legs. He clutched her foot against him for a second, then he reluctantly removed it. With care, he lowered her feet and slipped her shoes back on.

"Not that I don't appreciate foot jobs, Peaches, but the first time you make me come, I want to be fully seated inside your sweet cunt, with your screams ringing in my ears."

Her brain was frying, but she still managed to blurt out, "Umm... Peaches?"

His grin was wide and hot and so beautiful it made her chest ache just to see it. "That ass of yours makes me think of firm, succulent peaches. I can't wait to take my first bite."

She was still absorbing that when he adjusted himself,

speared a slightly shaky hand through his hair and stood. He gazed down at her, one hand held out.

The band was in the middle of a tune about a hot, sultry night when she placed her hand in his and left the club.

Tracy was waiting for her when she reached her suite, both Louis Vuitton weekenders Keely had insisted she take neatly arranged on a porter's cart.

The petite brunette's gaze swung between Zach and her, and Bethany caught a swiftly hidden look of envy as her eyes tracked Zach to his suite door.

She turned and caught Bethany's gaze, then quickly smiled. "It's been a pleasure being your hostess, Miss Green," she said, her tone betraying nothing but pure professionalism.

Bethany smiled around the weird feelings coursing through her. "Thank you, Tracy. I'm sorry I'm not staying for the full trip."

"That's okay. It'll be a pleasure to act as your hostess again if… I mean, *when* you join us for another trip."

Since there was zero chance of that happening again in this lifetime, Bethany merely smiled. Her smile widened when Philip emerged from Zach's suite, carrying large designer suitcases.

He exchanged a few words with Tracy before leading Bethany into the elevator.

Bethany turned as Zach came out. Immediately, she felt that knee-knocking zing of awareness and increased pulse rate that watching him move brought.

As if perfectly attuned to her, his head snapped up and his eyes clashed with hers.

A slow smile lifted his lips, and she forgot to breathe.

"I didn't realize Philip was seeing to you on this trip as well," she said.

"Philip has been seeing to me for over ten years," he replied.

Surprise made her steps falter. "But I thought he was my personal bodyguard."

"I may have made a few adjustments to the arrangements before we left New York."

"A few adjust— You mean you were so sure you'd achieve this end? That I'd come with you?"

"Not sure. Hopeful. Besides, I trust Philip. More than any other human being."

The unexpected insight into his life made her glance at him, and she held her breath as she waited for more.

But he merely stepped into the elevator and pushed the button for the first floor.

The limo ride to the airport was different from the ride that had brought them to the hotel from their tour.

With the business world up and active on the other side of the globe, Zach Savage went into full entrepreneurial mode. Earpiece in place, he fired up a laptop, murmured an excuse and then proceeded to make phone call after phone call all the way to the airport. He switched from French to English to German with a fluency that made her eyes widen in awe. He barely stopped to show his passport before he was back on the phone again.

They were leaving the VIP lounge to board their flight when he turned to her with those laser, peace-shattering eyes. "I apologize for this, but I'm trying to clear my schedule as much as possible before we land in Paris. Is that okay?"

The idea that a hot, deliciously sexy billionaire was asking her if it was okay to conduct business melted away the trace of irritation she'd been feeling. The thought that he was clearing his schedule just for her made her chest ache in an unfamiliar way. She reached for her purse.

"It's fine. Go ahead. I need to make some calls myself."

When he froze and raised an eyebrow, she answered, "My parents. I promised to get in touch when I landed in Shanghai." She also needed to let Keely know she was deviating from her once-in-a-lifetime experience.

As to whether Keely would root for her or not was another matter. For all her grab-life-by-the-balls attitude, Keely could be extremely grounded and conservative in certain situations.

She might not think Bethany was making a mistake by accepting whatever it was Zachary Savage was offering. Then again, she might.

Which was why Bethany chickened out after she'd finished speaking to her parents and sent her best friend a text instead of calling her. Although they were surprised about her abrupt change of plan, they accepted her breezy explanation about why she'd ditched The Indigo Lounge experience—she'd decided to join a friend in Paris and Morocco instead of finishing her trip.

She turned her phone off and followed Zachary Savage into first class. Noting that they were the only occupants, she turned to him. His gaze was firmly fixed on her as he conversed in fluent Italian, and he cut the connection only when a stewardess stepped forward and showed them to their seats. Bethany accepted her glass of chilled champagne and the chocolate truffles with a smile and tried not to look awestruck at her luxurious surroundings.

Zach broke his conversation long enough for takeoff. "Everything went well with your phone calls?"

"My parents don't know enough about my trip to question why I've descended into madness by abandoning it. All they want to know is that I'm safe."

He nodded. "Your safety is guaranteed. Never doubt that."

There was a depth of conviction in his tone that made her believe him. Taking a piece of chocolate, he fed it to her, watched her mouth with hungry, intense eyes as she chewed and licked her lips.

With what seemed like monumental effort, he pulled his gaze away and sat back in his chair. "Try and get some sleep, Peaches. You'll need your strength in the hours and days to come."

"Another boast, Savage?"

"A very friendly warning from a very hungry carnivore who intends to stop only when you're in danger of becoming permanently bow-legged," he said darkly. He took her almost empty glass of champagne, set it to one side. Then he shook out the softly luxurious cashmere throw the stewardess presented him with.

Before she could ask him what he was doing, he pressed a button on her seat and Bethany felt the seat recline with an almost silent whine.

When she was fully reclined, he placed the throw over her and tucked her in. He picked up the glass and raised an eyebrow at her.

She shook her head because she didn't need any more alcohol. Between the power of his words and gentleness of his touch, her whole body was buzzing.

This man was strong, powerful, but sensitive in a way that woke fear deep in her heart. If she wasn't careful, he could devastate her. Before he'd even laid a single finger on her.

He turned back to her and sent her one of those soul-melting smiles. Then, his earpiece back in place, he launched into another business conversation.

She tried to read a magazine for a while, then felt her lids beginning to droop. It was as she was falling asleep, nestled in the thick luxury of the cashmere throw, that the thought intruded.

She'd never asked him what he'd meant by when the time is right.

7

Her breath caught at the heart-stopping sight of the Eiffel Tower. Beside her, in the luxurious cocoon of his Maybach Laundaulet, Zachary turned to her and smiled, but there was a distance in his eyes—the same distance she'd noted when they'd landed half an hour ago—that made alarm tingle down her spine.

"Is this your first time in Paris?" he asked.

"No, my parents brought me here for my twenty-first. I promised myself I'd return one day." She didn't add that she'd promised to return with the man she loved. She'd thought for a long time that man would be Chris.

She pressed agitated hands on the soft white leather seat and forced the thought away. They were in the city made for lovers.

When, exactly, she and Zachary Savage would attain that status was beginning to loom like a specter of uncertainty in her mind. She glanced at him and noted his jaw was set harder than it had been minutes ago.

Was he worried about his meeting? Did the city hold memories in some way that didn't sit well with him?

"This isn't your first time, obviously," she ventured.

"No, it isn't. But I hope after today I can stay clear for a while."

She frowned. "Why would you want to stay clear?"

"I'm hoping to conclude my business today. Then there won't be any need to return."

His phone pinged with yet another phone call. The last twelve hours had shown her just how busy he was. His phone never stopped ringing. She was stunned he'd managed to keep it off while he'd toured Shanghai with her.

This time the conversation was conducted in low, seductive lilting French, which turned surprisingly clipped before he hung up.

"Everything okay?" she couldn't help asking. More and more she was realizing just how little she knew about him.

He turned those mesmerizing eyes on her but when he smiled, it looked strained. "Not yet, but I'll take care of it. We're here."

Her attention was drawn from him to their destination.

The Indigo Belle Plaza was even more breathtaking than the Indigo Shanghai had been. This building took up a proud and possessive corner of the Rue de Rivoli, with stunning historical architecture steeped in every stone. It exuded wealth and class in a way very few buildings could, from the porticoed windows to the indigo and French flags, fluttering together in the breeze from what looked like solid gold masts.

Her heart hammered as she was helped from the back seat by a starchily uniformed doorman. Just as in Shanghai, Zach was treated like royalty.

She watched, semi-bemused as the manager bowed and scraped them into the elevator that took them to the presidential suite.

They'd barely entered when Zach turned to her. That restless distance was still in place, making her heart pound with dread. Before she could summon the courage to ask him what was going on, he started to back away.

"Make yourself at home. Order room service. I will be back in a few hours."

"O... okay."

He started walking to the door and stopped, then spun on his heel. "And Bethany?"

"Yes?"

Weirdly, the sight of his clenched fists made her feel better. His gaze devoured her, frightening yet reassuring her that he was just as surely being driven insane by the sexual charge arcing between them. In that, she wasn't alone.

"Know this. Everything changes on my return."

* * *

Everything changes on my return.

The words reverberated in her head as the hours passed with excruciating slowness. She showered, she channel-hopped, she rearranged the meager clothes she'd packed.

Then she ordered the most heavenly burger and fries she'd ever tasted.

And still only two hours had passed.

Unable to sit still any longer, Bethany grabbed the glossy Hotel Guide. The boutiques listed in the shopping section had her springing up and snatching up her bag.

As she left the room, she thanked her stars she hadn't succumbed to Chris's pressure to use the nest egg she'd received from her grandparents for a deposit for a bigger apartment. Granted, using it to splurge on underwear for her tryst with a hot, sexy billionaire was not quite what she'd had in mind. But what the fuck, Chris-the-A-hole had left her in no doubt that the world could turn upside down and take a dump on her in a blink of an eye.

Go large or go home!

She bought six pairs of matching bras and panties from the first shop. Makeup with heavily accented tips on application came from the assistant in the second shop. But it was the third shop that took her breath away. The dresses were all in shades of indigo. Her heart hammered as she flicked through long evening dresses and short, casual, yet sophisticated, day wear. Touching the color that was so special to Zachary made her feel close to him.

Bethany wasn't sure how long she was in the shop but she began to notice the curious looks from the sales assistants.

After she was asked for a fifth time whether she needed help, she chose a short, lace dress that ended mid-thigh, along with a silk pantsuit and gold pumps, with hoop earrings to match.

Exiting, she dashed to the last shop, a perfumery, and stocked up on her favorite scents.

The porter was waiting by the doors and held it open for her. "I'll take your bags, ma'am."

She laughed. "I'm twenty-four. Ma'am-ing me hurts my feelings. And I can carry my own bags, thanks."

He nodded with a dignity that seemed at variance with his immense size. He summoned the elevator, and they rode to the penthouse in silence.

A quick glance at her watch as the elevator slid open showed she'd been downstairs two hours. With any luck, she didn't have much longer to wait till Zach—

"Where the hell have you been?"

Her bags fell from her hands.

He stood there, larger than life, eyes ablaze with hunger and... anxiety?

"You're back," she said stupidly, but once again, the sheer beauty of him had rendered her brains useless. And the fact that he'd been anxious about her sent a thrill of delight surging through her.

Then she noticed his clenched jaw and the whitened skin around his mouth. The guy was seriously riled.

"I thought you'd left."

She frowned. "Why would I leave?"

He clawed a hand through his hair. "I didn't intend to be away this long, and when I got back and you weren't here... I thought you'd changed your mind. You didn't tell Philip where you were going—"

"Because I only went downstairs to get a few things..."

His gaze left hers and skimmed over the shopping bags. But barely a second later, that unstoppable gaze was back on her, pinning her to the spot, stopping the breath in her lungs.

He sauntered forward. This time, his fists weren't clenched. And the look in his eyes had changed from hungry yearning to predatory warning. "You went shopping?"

She nodded, unable to speak past the crazy hammering of her heart.

"Philip would've gotten you anything you needed."

"I didn't... I was going stir crazy here. I just wanted to step out for a little while."

He reached her, walked past her and shut the door. The lock slid home with an ominous click that sent a shiver through her.

She felt him behind her, but his scent, his powerful aura, was all around her, reeling her in, claiming her. "You scared the shit out of me, Bethany."

"I didn't mean to."

"Be that as it may, I intend to make you pay for that. What was the last thing I said to you before I left, Bethany?" he growled in her ear.

"You... said... everything changes on your return?" she whispered.

"Yes, I did." Warm fingers touched her wrists and drifted up her arms in a whisper-thin caress that sent sensation rushing through her. "I've waited what seems like forever for this moment. And I come back to find you gone. Philip didn't know where you'd gone. Do you know what that did to me?" he murmured.

"N... no."

"I was desperate, Bethany. I saw all the plans I'd made going to shit."

"You made plans?" she asked breathlessly.

"A million. Ninety-nine percent of them involved the many and varied ways I was going to fuck you. If you'd run out on me, I'd have had no choice but to hunt you down." He laced his fingers through hers, brought both hands behind her back. "Because walking around another minute with this would've killed me." Still holding her hands, he placed hers directly over his cock as his teeth sank into the soft flesh of her shoulder.

She gasped as the thick, long ridge of his rock-hard cock filled her hands. Her fingers closed on him, and his deep moan echoed around the room. The ragged, masculine sound drenched her sex with heat. She tightened her grip, eager to hear it again.

He hissed in her ear and clamped his hands over hers. "Easy, baby. I haven't prematurely blown my load in a long time. But waiting this long to have you has driven me to the edge. It won't take much more to shove me over it." He eased her hands from him.

Fierce heat burned in his eyes, and the hunger stamped on his face stopped her breath. With a grunt, he pulled her close, slid powerful hands into her hair and angled it towards him.

"What did I say about kissing you?" he murmured, his breath hot against her lips.

"A… a kiss for every minute we've been together?"

"You remembered. Good girl."

His mouth was hard and demanding, his tongue a lash of pleasure that took over her senses in the blink of an eye. He sucked, he bit, he cajoled her into giving him more.

Before she could take another breath, Bethany found herself glued from breast to thigh against him. He devoured her mouth the way he'd promised to devour her body. Liquid oozed from between her sex as he feasted on her with a shameless desire that echoed the one rocking through her body.

When the need to breathe became paramount, he lifted his head. But only the barest inch, as if now that he'd given himself permission to touch, he couldn't bear to be more than a hairsbreadth away. He pressed his forehead to hers.

"Oh, sweet baby. I'm going to enjoy fucking you. I'm going to fuck you very hard for a very, very long time. And you're going to love every second of it."

His hands left her hair and drifted over her neck to her shoulders. He looked down, saw her hard, tight nipples and growled. "And when you're too tired to move, I'm going to suck on those pretty tits until you beg me to fuck you all over again."

He gripped her waist, swung her into his arms and headed for the large sofa in the living room. The early evening sunlight slanted into the room, casting it in a golden glow. All around them, Zachary's wealth and influence demanded awe and appreciation, but Bethany only had eyes for the stunningly gorgeous guy in front of her. The man who licked his lips as his gaze raked her from head to toe and back again.

She let her own gaze drift over him. The hard chest, which she'd felt under her hands a moment ago, lifted as he breathed. And below the belt of his trousers, his rigid erection was outlined, large and thick.

She went for his belt, unable to wait one moment longer to see his cock.

The need burning through her felt alien, raw, the anticipation almost painful.

"Bethany, wait."

She whimpered. "No, I don't want to wait. I want you. Inside me. Right now."

His jaw clenched, and his nostrils flared. "Shit."

"This wasn't part of your plan, was it?" A sense of power fizzed through her when she noticed the visibly shaking hand he clawed through his hair.

"I wanted to taste you all over, feast on that sweet cunt—"

"I want that too. But later. Please, Zach, you've made us wait for two days. Don't make me wait any longer."

"Bethany— Ah, fuck."

He ripped the dress she'd worn to go shopping downstairs from her body. Her simple cotton bra suffered the same fate. At the first sight of her bared breasts, he froze.

"Jesus. You're incredible." He lowered his head and ran his tongue over the upper slopes of her breasts, both hands cupping her and molding her as he grazed his teeth lightly over her flesh. He sucked a nipple into his mouth and moaned deep and long in appreciation. Several long flicks of his tongue, then he moved to the other breast and delivered the same treatment.

His moans of appreciation sent a fever of need through her. "God, you're so beautiful."

She swayed, and he clamped one arm around her waist, twisted her round and stretched her out on the sofa.

"I can't repay the compliment if you insist on being fully dressed."

His laugh was deep, rich and intensely arousing.

Bethany had never imagined she could get wet just from a man's laugh. But hearing Zachary laugh as he unbuttoned his shirt made her tingle even harder as liquid pleasure slicked her sex.

At the first sight of his smooth, chiseled chest, desire slammed through her. Her eyes widened as she took him in. His shoulders were powerful; easily fit enough to support her legs as he slammed into her. Arms, corded with sleek muscle, flexed as he reached for his zipper. His breathing turned ragged. When she looked into his eyes, his gaze was fixed on her.

"If you keep licking your lips like that when you watch my body, one of us will end up paying a very steep price."

With a start, Bethany realized that was exactly what she'd been doing. "I can't help it. You're gorgeous," she blurted.

He inhaled sharply, as if she'd surprised him. His movements were slightly jerky as he shucked off his shoes and socks and stepped out of his trousers.

Gloriously naked, Zachary Savage was a pure work of art. But Bethany's gaze was riveted on the heavy length of his cock, which he now gripped as he gazed hungrily down at her body.

Jesus, he was big! A spike of apprehension pierced her desire, causing a shiver to run through her body.

He noticed and stepped closer. Lowering himself over her, he kissed her, chasing the apprehension away. "You don't need to worry, beautiful Bethany. I'll take care of you."

As he sealed his mouth over hers, his hand slid over her breast. Pleasure ricocheted through her as he tweaked her nipple then drifted lower over her abdomen. Gentle fingers traced the seam of her panties then dipped downward.

One thick finger grazed her clit. Her hips jerked so violently, she almost dislodged his hand.

"Christ, you're so responsive," he groaned against her mouth, then dipped his finger again, teasing, torturing, delivering pleasure that sent fire rushing over her nerves.

His mouth left hers, nipping at her earlobe before sucking on it. Down below, his one finger joined the other and commenced a steady, relentless rhythm.

"Zach! Oh, God!" Her thighs shook then widened to accommodate him, her hips rocking in a rhythm of their own as her pleasure escalated.

Zach's mouth trailed lower, captured one nipple and pulled it deep into his mouth. She cried out as his thumb replaced his finger in an ever-increasing friction that made stars explode behind her eyelids. One finger dipped inside her pussy. Her muscles clenched immediately around him, gripping with wild need as blistering hunger tore through her.

"What a greedy cunt you have. Do you want more? Do you want another finger? Hmm?" His tongue swirled around her wet nipple, his hot breath washing over her flesh as he spoke.

"Yes! Please... yes."

"Greedy girl. My lovely, greedy, exquisite Peaches." He finger-fucked her slowly as the words tumbled from his lips.

But still he only used one finger.

"Zach..."

"Tell me what you want, baby."

"More... I want more of that."

One finger joined the other. Her muscles stretched as her hips rode him faster, faster, her breath coming in choppy sobs.

When her head started to thrash on the cushion, he speared his fingers into her hair and held her still.

"Look at me, Bethany. I want to see how fantastic you look when you come."

Her mouth dropped open in a gasp as sensation rocked through her.

Silver eyes speared hers, giving her no chance of looking away. Expert fingers sank deeper into her, curling just at the right angle to hit her where she needed it most.

She screamed as the first wave caught her.

"Fuck, yeah. That's it. Give it up for me, Peaches."

Her hips bucked wildly as a tidal wave of pleasure ripped through her. Without breaking eye contact, he lowered his head and took one nipple between his teeth, biting down on the hard tip. She came harder, unbelievably finding her orgasm prolonged as he tortured her flesh.

He pulled his fingers out of her and used the pad of his hand to smear the slick wetness over her sex. Then he went to work again, rubbing her whole sex with a firm pressure that made her pulse spike higher.

"Jesus... Zach... I can't..."

"Yes, you can. Just immerse yourself in it, baby. Your body is dying to experience it again. See how your hips are fucking my hand?"

Shocked, she looked down and watched her hips roll into his hand in perfect symmetry to his rubbing. "Don't deny yourself. Just let it go."

Her body felt light and leaden all at once. Her breasts ached with a need so acute that she cupped them to ease the pain.

"God, yes. Play with them. Show me how you'll cup them for me when I put my cock between them."

Dirty words had never been in her sexual repertoire. But

suddenly Bethany couldn't get enough. She showed him what he wanted. His breath hissed out, his eyes darkening with stark need as she caught her nipples between her fingers and teased them. He licked his lips again as she squeezed tighter.

Heat gripped her abdomen as the onslaught of another orgasm slammed into her. Overwhelmed by the intensity of it, her eyes started to drift shut.

"Bethany!" His voice was a sharp command.

Panting, she raised her eyes to his. "I'm coming... Oh, God, please... I'm coming!"

"Watch me, baby. See how much I love watching you come."

He rubbed harder, his eyes darkening and his mouth dropping open as her pleasure became his. Plumping her clit over and over, he drew every ounce of sensation from her. Through it all, he kept his eyes locked on hers, his teeth savaging his lower lip as he lost himself in her pleasure.

The emotion that he drew from her was so intense, tears spiked her eyes as she climaxed. Her scream ended in a sob, her shaking uncontrollable, as he gathered her into his arms.

"Oh, God," she murmured, unable to stop the tremors.

"Shhh, baby." He smoothed his hand down her sides for long minutes, soothing her until she was mindless, floating on a sea of post-orgasmic bliss. "Relax back on the sofa and spread your legs wider for me. I'm going to lick you now."

Bethany jerked, her comfort and peace shot to pieces at the image that slammed into her head. "What?"

He reared over her, big and powerful and so impossibly beautiful, and renewed shock slammed through her at the thought that she was really here, with him.

"I've been dying to taste you since you walked into my office two days ago. Don't ask me to wait any longer."

He started to lower her soaked panties.

"Zach, I can't… I'm not…"

"It's okay, I know you're not ready yet. I won't make you come again just yet. You'll enjoy it, I promise." He pulled her panties off and tossed them away.

As he rearranged himself between her thighs, Bethany's gaze slid to the rock-hard erection that almost touched his navel.

"You made me think you were right on the edge. But you're not, are you?"

His smile was wicked and stunningly gorgeous. "You have no idea how close I am, baby. But making you come and witnessing your pleasure was more important to me. I just want to make you happy."

Her breath caught at the simple, powerful words.

She looked around in a daze as Zach lifted one of her legs and draped it over the top of the sofa.

How the hell had she lucked out like this? What had she done to deserve one of the most virile, mesmerizingly beautiful men in the world, preparing to lick her to the brink of another orgasm?

His dark head lifted suddenly and he locked his gaze on hers. "What are you thinking?"

"I'm wondering what the hell did I do to deserve you?" she blurted.

He squeezed her thigh and looked down at her exposed sex. "Fuck, no. That should be my thought. Because you're a prize any man would kill for, Bethany. But you're here, right now, with me."

"Not every man," she said, the pain of memory ripping through her. When he tensed, she cursed herself for being unable to totally push away the unwanted ghosts, for ruining this incredible moment.

But it was too late. Zachary's eyes had sharpened with interest.

"Who was he?" he asked as he arranged her other leg over the wide seat.

"Nobody... He was..."

"Tell me," he insisted, his hard hands squeezing her thigh in deadly command.

"His name was... is Chris. We went to college together. Moved to New York together. I thought we were... we would be..."

"He hurt you?"

Breath shaking out, she tried to look away, but his gaze compelled hers. "Yes. He hurt me very badly."

"Fuck him. He's an asshole for letting you go..." His heated gaze slid over her, until it burned between her legs again. "For letting this go, but I'm glad he's gone. Because you're mine now. All mine." The possessiveness in his tone would've shocked her, had she not been in a daze. "Say it, Bethany."

"I'm... I'm yours," she whispered.

Satisfaction spread over his face as he lowered his body between her legs. He slid his hands under her hips until he gripped her waist from beneath. The sight of his powerful hands holding her down for his ministrations blew her mind.

Of course, it was nothing compared to the first, lazy slide of his tongue up the wall of her sex, or the sheer pleasure on his face as he licked his lips at the first taste of her.

"Fucking gorgeous. Christ, Peaches, I could eat you all day."

She felt her blush wash over her chest and shoot up into her face. He laughed at her embarrassment and resumed licking her. He was careful to avoid her clit, already so attuned to her that he knew one touch would send her rocketing sky high. Not a bad thing, but she was genuinely scared another orgasm this soon would blow her wide open.

Zach was right. His languid attention brought her pulse rate down enough for her to enjoy watching what he was doing to her. Time ceased to matter as he pleasured her with slow, sure strokes.

After what seemed an age, he kissed the inside of her thigh and quirked an eyebrow at her. "Feeling better?"

"Yes... I like that. It feels nice."

He smiled, his tension from earlier gone. "I know. But I'm going to fuck you now, baby. It'll feel nice, too. I promise."

8

Before she could respond, he plunged two fingers inside her. Her hips arched off the sofa as sensation ramped up high, higher than before.

He lapped her clit with his tongue while he flexed his fingers, stretching her. Readying her for his possession.

With his free hand, he lazily plucked a packet from his trouser pocket.

Eyes on her, he flared the condom over the wide, engorged head of his cock in one slick move.

It struck her how practiced he seemed at that maneuver, but the thought was washed away a second later when his fingers slid out of her and plunged back in.

"You're so wet for me," he crooned with satisfaction. "So gorgeous."

He finished rolling on the condom and stretched over her, his golden body a stunning landscape that dried her mouth. When he fused his mouth to hers, Bethany immediately opened, her need for him bordering on insanity.

The wide crown of his cock nudged her and she shuddered. "Zach..."

"I love the way you say my name. You moan it in a way that makes me want to fuck it out of you again and again."

"Do it. Now," she begged.

"Ah, darling. How can I resist an invitation like that, hmm?"

He slid into her, one perfect inch at a time until she was stretched so tight that she hovered on the border between pleasure and pain.

"I'll take care of you, Bethany. But you need to tell me if it gets too much, okay?"

Pleasure screaming through her, she nodded. She gripped his hips as he pressed into her, undulating in a stunningly smooth motion that made her even more wet.

Her renewed slickness made him groan. "Jesus, you know what that does to me?" he moaned.

Plunging deeper, he buried himself almost to the hilt. No matter how long he'd prepared her, she still couldn't take all of him. When she whimpered, he drew back but immediately, she felt empty. "No! Please, give it to me."

He slid himself back into her tight sheath, causing another shudder to rake through her as he stretched her.

"You love what I'm doing to you?"

"God... yes! It's... You're unbelievable."

He captured her hands in his and placed them above her head while he sucked her lower lip into his mouth. "Good, things are about to get a whole lot nicer."

His cocky reassurance pulled a choked laugh out of her, even as her pulse shot up once again.

Zachary Savage fucked like he had all the time in the world. Sure, long, expert strokes that left a trail of fire all the way along her passage, a fire he had every intention of stoking with each lazy stroke. He licked her lower lip, then grazed his way to her jaw before capturing one earlobe. A quick bite had her gasping for breath.

"Jesus. Is there any part of you that doesn't respond to my touch? On second thought, don't answer that. I want to find out for myself."

His strokes increased in frequency, her hitched cries seeming to excite him. But still he maintained absolute control over his strokes.

Beneath him, sensation built. Heat flooded her, burning, consuming her as his cock filled her with each thrust. "Zach... I don't know how much more I can take. I want... I want..."

"Not yet." He sealed his mouth over hers, licked his tongue into her mouth before releasing her. "Let me fuck you some more. Just a little while longer. You feel so good, baby. So soft."

Bethany wondered how he could keep such expert control when she could already feel her mind beginning to fracture as pleasure consumed her. The stark hunger on his face told another story. He was intent on devouring her, on extracting every single ounce of pleasure from her. Then extracting some more.

The idea that he wanted her this much blew her mind. But the evidence was right there in his face. He was as insane with pleasure as she was, his sculpted chest beginning to expand and contract as he took increasingly rapid breaths.

"Put your legs around me." She complied but he shook his head, his eyes blazing a savage demand. "Tighter. I want to feel your legs gripping me the way your hungry cunt is gripping my cock."

Her thighs shook as she clenched them tight. The move forced him deeper into her on the next stroke, taking pleasure to a whole new level.

Her jagged scream made his eyes darken. "Tell me how that feels."

"Incredible. Oh, God, Zach, more, please, fuck me harder!"

Her throaty demand seemed to crack the last of his control. One hand still trapping hers above her head, he gripped her ass with the other and slammed into her.

His lips parted on a pained grimace as he increased his thrusts. Perspiration sheened both their bodies as they writhed together, racing towards the promise of mind-blowing release.

"Bethany! Fuck!"

He slammed into her, harder than before. She screamed, her lids heavy from near-delusional pleasure.

"No, baby," he commanded. "Eyes on me. Watch what you do to me. See how insane fucking you has driven me."

His eyes were crazy with lust, flames bursting through as stark need clenched his jaw tight.

"Oh," she gasped, so unbelievably turned on by the knowledge of what she'd done to him that she screamed harder.

His smile was almost sadistically smug. "Like that, do you? Do you love that you have me at your mercy? Do you love knowing that I'd rather die than stop now? That I'd rather stop breathing than stop fucking you right now?"

"Yes! Oh, God..." The orgasm took her by surprise even though she'd known she was close. It rippled through her like the beginnings of an earthquake. All the way down her spine to coil tight within her belly. He drank her keening moan with a searing kiss.

"Just like that baby. I'm so close."

His nostrils pinched together as he reared back and hooked his gaze on hers.

"Zach!"

"Yes, Peaches. Now! Right fucking now!"

He slammed into her once, twice. His teeth bared on a savage growl as her orgasm ripped through her. Spasming wildly beneath him, Bethany heard her screams echo through the large room and bounce off the walls.

"Jesus!" His gorgeous hair fell over his forehead, framing his stunning face as he bucked wildly on top of her, spurting his long, endless release inside her.

The pleasure-pain reflected in his eyes made her want to touch him, kiss him. When she struggled against his hold, he finally set her free.

Pushing his hair back, she levered herself up and kissed his mouth, her eyes still wide open and connected with his. His groan was long and deep, the connection searing, unlike anything she'd ever experienced before.

A feeling of vulnerability crept over her. Absurdly, she felt as if Zach was looking deep into her soul and allowing her a glimpse into his. She saw beauty, pleasure... and pain.

He broke the connection first, his head dropping down until his forehead touched hers. Their breaths mingled as he slid his arms around her shoulder and pulled her close.

Her thighs shook with tension and she loosened her hold on him.

"Did I say you could let me go?" he demanded, but his lips curved in a smile against her shoulder.

"I'm so liquid right now, not all the ballet training in the world can make me keep this pose."

His head slowly lifted, his eyes gleaming with keen interest. "You're a trained ballerina?"

"Was. Unfortunately, my ass started to grow when I was fourteen and hasn't stopped growing. I had to give up hopes of becoming a world-famous prima ballerina and settle for being a not-so-world-famous events organizer."

His interest grew. “So just how... flexible are you?” The question was so blatantly sexual that her barely lowered pulse spiked higher again.

“Why do you want to know?” she asked, despite the blush creeping over her skin.

“Because I want to know just how... adventurous we can get together.” Lust slid over his face. He licked his lips in a purely predatory way that made her stomach muscles clench hard.

Unbelievably, he started to get hard again inside her.

At her shaky breath, he grimaced. “Let’s continue this in the shower. I want to know all about your dreams of becoming a ballerina. And the hot topic of your ass growing.”

He laughed at the glare she gave him. A moment later, they both groaned as he pulled out of her.

Zach reared back and looked down her pink sex. “You’re so fucking beautiful down there. I could eat you all over again.”

Her visible shudder made him laugh, even as he drifted his knuckles over her still tingling sex.

“But first, a shower. And some food for you.”

He stood up and held out his hand to her.

As Bethany followed his tall, lean body, she tried to make sense of the myriad emotions tumbling through her.

She’d just experienced the most incredible sexual episode of her life. Elation, confusion and trepidation fought within her.

* * *

Zach sensed her roiling emotions as he led her to the bathroom.

Heck, he was still reeling from what had just happened on the living room sofa. He’d never come so hard for so long.

And that command for her to look into his eyes as he came?

Where the hell had that come from? The last thing he wanted was for any woman to look into his soul.

The blackness of his soul and the barren echoes of pain that had been a part of him for so long he hardly noticed them anymore—these were the last things he wanted to share with Bethany; this sweet, slightly vulnerable yet brave woman who hadn't run a mile when she'd caught a glimpse of the sort of man he was underneath the civilized gloss.

But somehow, in fucking Bethany, the need to connect with her at that point had become visceral, necessary. His need for her had certainly been enough to propel him onto an Indigo Lounge trip after he'd sworn never to set foot on one of his planes again.

And, boy, had it almost blown his cock off with the intensity of it.

His cock, which had woken again when she'd mentioned her ass and her former intention to be a ballerina, grew harder.

As they passed a large cheval mirror, he glanced at her reflection, saw her flushed body still sweaty from their exertions and fought not to flatten her against the wall and fuck her all over again.

Time, she needed a little time to recover.

Truth be told, so did he.

He still hadn't shaken off the residual panic he'd felt when he'd returned to find her gone. The sense of loss and disappointment had been so acute he'd wondered whether he'd lost his mind. He'd been in the process of calling his security people to track her down when she'd turned up. That in itself stunned the hell out of him.

When had he felt strongly enough about any woman to track her down after she'd walked away from him?

Never.

And yet, the thought of Bethany Green, a woman he'd known for barely two days, walking away from him—

Soft hands touched his back, and his mind melted.

Whirling, he faced her in front of the mirror.

Blue eyes, lightening now she wasn't caught in the maelstrom of sensation, stared up at him. When they dropped to his mouth, heat shot into his groin.

The unabashed way she wanted him excited him more than he'd been excited in a very long time. Her eyes flicked to his again, and he saw the hesitation in their depths.

He cupped her face and tilted her head up. "You don't have to be afraid to tell me what you want, Bethany. You hold nothing back between us. If you want to kiss me, you kiss me. Whatever you want, you take it. Because I sure as hell won't be holding back when it comes to you. Understood?"

Her eyes widened, this time with excitement and a hint of that trepidation he'd seen earlier. Whatever her asshole ex had done to her, the bastard had made her doubt her sexuality and femininity. He barely stopped himself from cursing and waited for her to answer. When she didn't, he passed his thumb over her lower lip. Felt it tremble beneath his touch.

"Bethany? Tell me what you want."

She sucked in a huge breath. "You. I want you so badly I can't understand it. We just had sex, and yet I want you again. Like right now—"

Relief smashed through his chest. Sex he could deal with, even if this brand of crazy sex held something new he wasn't altogether familiar with.

Grinning, he kissed her. "Glad you feel that way, baby. I wouldn't want you to think I was a crazy sex-obsessed monster who devours orgasms for breakfast."

"Sex god."

"Excuse me?"

"Sex god. That's what I thought you were the moment I saw you."

He felt his grin widen. "And I thought you were going to leave before I got the chance to get my mouth on that juicy cunt of yours."

Her husky laugh made him harder. "You thought I would leave?"

"You stood in that goddamn doorway for so long, I thought you'd turned into a statue. Then you walked in and Johnny Boy Band got his horn-dog eyes on you. I wanted to smash his teeth in."

"Jax is a sweet guy."

An unpleasant feeling threatened to ruin his mood. "He wanted to fuck you. I wanted to smash his face in."

Her smile dimmed a little, and he realized he'd nearly growled his response. But he didn't take it back. The parts of himself he could reveal to Bethany needed to be revealed up close and immediately. He didn't want there to be any misapprehension when it came to what he wanted.

"Does that worry you?" he asked, holding his breath for her answer.

"I don't know. No one's felt that way about me before." Again, pain shadowed her eyes.

Again, he fought back his curse. "I feel that way about you now. I'm insanely possessive about you. The thought of any other guy getting close to this"—he pulled back to gaze over the perfection of her body—"makes me insane."

"We've known each other barely two days, Zach."

"I knew how I felt before I even saw your face."

Her breath fractured. "What... what are you saying?"

"That I don't know what the hell this is. But no other guy is going to come near you while we figure it out."

"And how exactly are we going to figure it out? I don't even know where you live or if I'll see you again once this trip is over."

"You'll see me. That I can promise you."

Questions filled her eyes. Questions he wasn't ready to answer because he hadn't figured out the answers yet. And especially when his cock was fired up strongly enough to hammer nails. Tugging her after him, he resumed his journey down the hallway.

Her fingers jerked in his when they entered the bathroom. He glanced at her to find her eyes riveted on the wide bath, her features pale.

"What is it?"

"I don't do bathtubs..."

Zach tugged her close and drifted his mouth over her jaw and neck. "For what I have in mind, the shower is better."

He felt her relief and pulled back. "What exactly do you have against bathtubs?"

She shook her head, her hands sliding up his chest as she leaned in closer. "I don't want to talk about it right now, if you don't mind?"

"I do mind. But I'll let you distract me with those delicious nipples you're rubbing against my chest."

He walked backward with her into the immense shower, programmed the temperature settings on the electronic panel and turned on the large square showerhead. Six jets spewed warm water into the space where he directed them. He glanced over to the wide bench on the far side of the shower enclosure and dismissed it.

That would come later. For now, he had a more urgent wish.

"I've frisked that tight, plump ass of yours. I've held it as I fucked you on the sofa. But I haven't actually seen it naked yet. So, Bethany Green, how about you turn around and show me that hot little ass of yours, huh?"

* * *

"There's nothing little about it," Bethany replied, the old insecurity about her ass rising to the fore, despite the hungry heat in Zach's eyes. "It's ridiculously large."

"Show me." His hand drifted to his cock and grasped it. Bethany watched, mesmerized as he caressed it lazily, his tongue darting out to touch his lower lip.

The motion of him stroking his cock was so hypnotizing, she locked her knees to keep from sliding into a stupid puddle of need. When he made his demand again, she shook her head. He was so gorgeous and she... she couldn't turn around.

"Zach..."

"Turn the fuck around. Now." The demand was rough. Urgent.

Steam rose in the room, unfortunately not enough to provide any camouflage. But it was enough to raise her already soaring temperature.

"You make me come over there and you'll regret it," he warned.

She squeezed her eyes shut for several seconds. Then, slowly she turned, presenting her back and her worst feature to the probing gaze of the most beautiful man in the world.

Silence.

More silence.

Then... "Jesus, Bethany... How can you think...? Fuck!"

Her head whipped back, damp hair clinging to her cheeks as her gaze sought his. But he wasn't staring into her face. His gaze was riveted on her ass, a look so reverent, so intensely awed, that it weakened her knees.

He couldn't possibly love her ass... could he?

One step was all it took to bring him within touching distance of her. Instead, he reached up to one side of the showerhead and plucked a bottle off the shelf. Bethany didn't care what it contained. She couldn't look away from the stark hunger stamped on his face.

He flicked open the top with his thumb and tilted the bottle.

Cool liquid landed on her lower back, making her gasp at the contrasting sensations.

Still, without taking his eyes from her ass, he caressed his hand over his cock one more time, then began spreading the liquid all over her wet globes.

Sensation shot through her, which had nothing to do with his heated touch, although that in itself threatened to blow her mind.

"What... what is that?"

"Shhh, don't speak right now, baby. I'm in ass heaven."

"Seriously? Ass heaven?"

He slapped her ass hard enough to sting, then groaned. "God, I just made your ass pink." He slapped it again for good measure then reverently rubbed the lotion in, squeezing and caressing her flesh over and over.

With each caress, she felt her sex dampen, liquid heat oozing to join the cream of her earlier orgasm, making her slicker than she'd ever been in her life.

When Zachary gave an animalistic growl, she groaned with the eroticism of it. That finally drew his attention. Whatever he saw on her face made his silver eyes darken. He jerked forward and pressed his chest into her back. His growing stubble grazed her cheek as his sharp teeth caught her earlobe.

"Remember what I said about putting my cock between these sweet globes?"

"Yes?"

"Brace your hands on the wall, Peaches. I'm about to make good on my promise."

She braced. He stepped forward.

The feeling of his hot, velvety, stiff cock sliding between her ass cheeks was the most sensational feeling in the world. Bethany's mouth dropped open as her thighs trembled with the strength of her feelings.

"Jesus... How...?"

Zach gave a broken half laugh, half groan. "You feel it, too. It's insane how good it feels, isn't it?"

He pressed himself more deeply between her globes, slid his cock up and down. She'd never guessed how sensitive she was until she felt his cock head caress the space between her pussy and anus. At the first pass of his crown against her tight opening, she jerked as a different sensation spilled over her.

"You like that?"

"It feels... different."

He slid over the entrance again, pressing the ridged and veined underside of his cock against her. Again, sensation weakened her knees.

The thought had never even occurred to her that she could like anal play. Despite her close relationship with her vibrator, she'd never been bold enough to venture past her pussy.

Now insanely erotic, and God, yes, frightening thoughts tumbled through her head.

Could she...?

She shook her head to dispel the thought. Zach laughed as if he'd read her mind.

"What are you thinking of, naughty girl?"

"Umm... nothing," she gasped as he increased his pace.

"Keep thinking those thoughts. Watching you blush all over makes me harder."

She glanced around wildly, looking for something solid to hold on to.

"God, I love your ass. The way it cradles my cock. Look over your shoulder, baby, watch how great your ass looks."

She glanced down over her shoulder and nearly lost her mind at the sight of Zach's cock cradled between her butt cheeks. Her nipples tightened harder and her sex grew wetter, plumper with need.

His large hands gripped her hips, holding her steady as he pumped harder. The rough passes over her tight anus made her cry out. Unbelievably, she felt an orgasm creep closer.

"Oh!"

He pressed her forward until her nipples grazed the cool tiles with each thrust. Cold at her front, hot at her back. The contrasting sensations pulled her closer to the edge.

Zach's ragged breathing told her he was close too. "Fuck, Peaches. This feels even better than I imagined."

"Hmmm." She couldn't form coherent sentences any more than she could stop the climax that encroached.

Releasing her hips, he cupped her jaw with one hand, and with the other, he slid his fingers down her stomach to tease her clit.

The pressure on her jaw increased, forcing her mouth open. Still fucking her butt cheeks, he slowly slid two fingers inside her sweet heat and two in her mouth.

"Suck," he instructed.

Too much. Way too much sensation tumbled her over the edge. As her cheeks hollowed from sucking his fingers, Bethany clamped her eyes shut and moaned her fiery hot release.

Several seconds later, Zach buried his face in her shoulder and shouted his own release as he spurted his hot semen all over her ass.

Strong arms banded around her as the showerheads jetted over them. When they could move without the aid of the shower wall, he grabbed another bottle, this time a shower gel. He washed her from head to toe, then washed himself before turning off the shower. She turned to grab a towel, presenting him with her back once more.

His groaned hiss made her freeze.

"Ah, Peaches, I can't wait to show you my toy room in Marrakech."

9

He was the most gorgeous man in the world. And he loved her ass.

Bethany suppressed an insanely elated giggle and looked up to find him watching her over the candle-lit dinner table. They were on their own private terrace high enough up to provide the utmost privacy. Paris twinkled below them, a carpet of lights and moving cars. Over Zach's shoulder, the brilliantly lit iconic Eiffel Tower looked almost close enough to touch.

But it was the man who captivated her.

He wore black jeans and an indigo T-shirt that did amazing things to his eyes. His hair, still slightly damp from the shower, gleamed in the low light, and she had to stop herself from reaching out to smooth back the thick swathe that caressed his forehead.

She'd learned very quickly that touching Zach hampered clear thinking. She'd barely made it into one of the short, white, off-the-sleeve sundresses she'd packed after casually caressing his chest as he'd walked past her in the bedroom.

He'd imprisoned her against the bedpost and proceeded to

devour her mouth. The only thing that had saved her from another marathon sex session had been the loud growling of her ravenous stomach.

Zach had ordered an oyster starter for them, followed by steaks with fries and salad for himself, and a pasta carbonara for her. The accompanying Chardonnay had been heavenly, but it was the man sitting across from her who continued to make her insides zing every time she looked at him.

"What are you thinking?" she blurted, then kicked herself. She'd read in a magazine once that asking a man what he was thinking was asking to be hurt. She'd known him barely two days, but she already knew Zachary Savage had the power to hurt her. Even more than Chris had managed to hurt her with his gender-preference bullshit.

"I'm thinking about a lot of things, but mostly, I'm thinking… thirty minutes."

"Thirty minutes?"

"Yep. That's all that could've prevented this from happening." He gestured between them, his gaze never leaving her face. "I don't believe in coincidence or karma or any of that crap. But I can't help thinking I was there, in New York, for a reason. Because now this has happened, I can't imagine how the rest of my life would have been without this experience."

Just like that, he'd floored her. Tears sprang to her eyes and she hurriedly blinked them away.

She swallowed. Then swallowed again, but the lump in her throat refused to move.

She spoke around it. "For a guy who doesn't believe in karma, that's a lot of responsibility to lay at the feet of coincidence."

"I have a feeling I'd have met you again at some point. Sooner or later."

"And how do you figure that?"

He shrugged. "You work in events organizing. I have several companies that use New York organizers."

"That's still a stretch."

"So you think this was destiny?"

What had happened between them—and was happening—felt too powerful to be anything casual. And to be honest, it scared the hell out of her. "I don't know. Maybe."

"Whatever it is, I'm glad it happened now."

"Why?"

"You prefer that we would've met when I was ninety and couldn't fuck more than once a week?"

She laughed. "I guess not." She took another bite of her food and chewed, supremely conscious that he was still staring at her. Bethany wondered if she'd ever get used to Zach's unashamedly invasive stare whenever they were in the same room. It was almost as if he wanted to burrow under her skin and learn her every secret.

The weird thing was that a part of her wanted to hand him that freedom.

"So thirty minutes, and you would have been headed where exactly?" she asked.

He sipped his wine before answering. "San Francisco. That's where I'm based. I have a house in the Palisades. We stopped in Newark to refuel."

"Why San Francisco? Is that where you grew up?"

"No." His eyelids descended, veiling the look in his eyes. When he raised them again, his expression was carefully neutral. "I grew up in Louisiana."

His voice cautioned her not to probe any further. Despite the keen curiosity that assailed her, she heeded it. There was a reason Zachary Savage guarded his privacy so rabidly. Out of this world sex didn't give her the right to know his every secret or vice versa. Although there was one thing she was curious about.

"Why indigo?" she asked. "Is that your favorite color?"

One corner of his mouth lifted in a smile that was off-the-scale sexy. Her insides clenched harder. "Partly. Indigo is my middle name."

Her mouth dropped open. "No way. Your name is Zachary Indigo Savage? Were your parents hippies or something?"

The smile disappeared. "Yeah... something like that. Can we change the subject?" Dark grey eyes speared her, one brow raised in a way that said the question mark tagged at the end of the sentence was only a formality. A spurt of anger swirled through her.

"We can, but you need to know upfront. I don't like secrets. My ex kept a huge secret from me and made me believe we were solid when we weren't—"

"I told you he was a fool."

"Be that as it may, I'd rather not have another bombshell dropped at my feet when I least expect it. If you don't want me to get to know you better, that's fine. I like to think my instincts are savvy enough that I'm not sleeping with an axe murderer or a puppy-kicking sadist. But I want some reassurances that nothing we're doing right now will have any repercussions for my future."

"I can guarantee you that I've never kicked a puppy in my life, and I don't own an axe, none that I've personally wielded anyway. As for the rest, nobody can guarantee that, Peaches. But I can give you certain reassurances."

"Like what?" she pressed.

"Like exclusivity. And the knowledge that nothing in my past will directly affect you in any harmful way."

"And indirectly?"

He shrugged. "I try to keep my private life private, but I don't always succeed. Not with modern technology as pervasive as it is. The media might find out you're connected to me. Would that bother you?"

"That depends. Do you want me to remain your dirty little secret?"

He took another sip and licked a drop of wine from his lips in a way that made her want to leap over the table and devour every inch of his mouth, then work the rest of his body over well and good until he was as needy as she was.

"Peaches, I want you as dirty as I can get you, soaking wet and often."

A blush crawled over her face. "That's not what I meant and you know it."

He shrugged. "The tabloids make up stories that can sometimes be hurtful. I've grown immune to it to some extent, but you need to be prepared."

"What exactly do I need to be prepared for?"

"They may try and dig into your background, find out who you are, and use that to define your position in my life."

"So if they find out I'm just an ordinary girl who grew up in Upstate New York, they might conclude I'm some sort of gold digger trying to sink my claws into you?"

"It may not be that bad. It may be that they conclude I'm taken by a completely extraordinary girl whose body makes my head spin and my cock harder than ever."

Heat engulfed her, but the anxiety rushing through her stomach didn't go away. "But most likely it'll be the former."

He gave a single serious nod, his eyes narrowing on her face. "Can you handle that?"

She licked her lips and tried to shrug it away. "Maybe I won't need to. I only agreed to go to Marrakech with you. If we end things after that—"

"We won't," he inserted calmly as he topped up her wine.

Her heart did that stupid bouncy thing in her chest that left her breathless. "What makes you so sure?"

"Peaches, you're wasting time pursuing the wrong line of argument. We won't be over after Marrakech. Not by a long shot. That I can promise you. I can also guarantee you privacy there. It's what happens when we get back to the States that you need to worry about."

She played with the last mouthful of pasta on her plate. "But you live in San Francisco. I live in New York. How's that going to work?"

"I can work from anywhere in the world. Plus, I have a very large private plane, several cars and an adequately working cellphone. We'll work it out."

Her worry didn't abate. Slowly, she set her fork down. "Zach... This is going too fast. I don't know if I..."

He got up and came round to where she sat. Sinking down onto his heels, he grabbed her hips and swiveled her chair to face him.

"Do me a favor. Close your eyes and imagine your life a week from now. Then imagine it a month from now," he instructed softly, but with enough steel to let her know he was serious. Her heart did another of those stupid somersaults. "Do you want me in it?"

She found herself nodding before he'd even finished speaking. "Yes, I do."

He kissed her mouth, then kept the pressure until she opened for him. The tip of his tongue touched hers, flicked in erotic exploration before licking its way deeper. At her needy moan, he pulled back.

"Then that's all that matters." One hand drifted over her hip to brush against her crotch. It was the lightest of touches, but it still sent her pulse sky high. "This is all that matters."

"Great sex is all that matters?" A sliver of hurt cut through her.

"Great sex is an outstanding start. That was the reason you joined The Indigo Lounge trip, wasn't it?"

"I... Not really. I wanted to see what the experience was all about."

"So you weren't looking to connect with anyone?" He grated the words as if they soured his mouth.

"I don't know. Maybe..."

"Whatever the circumstances, we found each other. The only difference here is you're having the experience with me instead of some other guy whose face I'm trying very hard not to imagine. And it won't end once my plane lands back in Newark. Amongst other things, I promised you Bora Bora, remember?"

She nodded slowly. Although she felt somewhat appeased, Bethany couldn't shake the roller-coaster feeling undulating through her. But then he kissed her again. The effect of Zach Savage's mouth on her was a lesson in how devastating chemistry could be.

He wiped her out with just one touch of his lips on hers. When he raised his head several minutes later, she was on the edge of her chair, clinging to his shoulders. His body was firmly wedged between hers, her legs curled around his hips.

They both looked down. Her dress had ridden up to reveal her naked thighs, and his visibly erect hard-on was pressed against her damp panties. He rocked his hips and the friction electrified her swollen clit.

"God!"

He laughed. "I think my point is made, don't you?"

Extracting himself from her hands and legs, he readjusted her clothing, returned to his seat, refilled her almost empty glass and picked up his.

"Tell me about your job. Do you love what you do?"

Right. She was supposed to conduct a coherent conversation while she hovered on the brink of yet another orgasm?

She dragged desperate fingers through her hair. "I… umm… I guess. I have a degree in hospitality, and events organizing seemed the perfect choice when I graduated."

"Why the perfect choice?" he asked.

"My grandmother owned a B&B in Connecticut when I was young. I spent my summers there when I was a child and loved making up games and activities for the families that came there. It seemed a natural choice when it came to a career."

"Is Neon your first job?"

She looked up in surprise. "How do you know where I work?"

"You filled in your personal details when you applied to join Indigo."

"Oh. Yes, I joined as a junior organizer three years ago and was promoted to an account holder last year, before…"

"Before what?"

She thought for a moment and shrugged. There was no harm in letting him know she'd known about him before she joined his trip. "My bosses wanted your business. They asked me to investigate you. Find out if any of your business interests coincided with ours. But the companies you use are in the mega league. When I reported back that I couldn't find a way in, I stymied my prospects at Neon for a while."

"Ah, so our meeting wasn't karmic after all?" He sounded faintly disappointed and the look he gave her was mildly calculating.

"What, you think...? I had no idea you would be in Newark! And my presence on the Indigo trip had nothing to do with work. Besides, considering you had over five thousand applicants to choose from, it would've been a huge gamble to take, just on the off chance that I would be chosen."

"But you were."

"Would you rather you hadn't met me?"

"I think we've established my feelings on that point. But I'm wondering what you'd have done if the opportunity had arisen...?" he pressed.

She set her glass down. "Zach, I make it a point never to sleep with a client, potential or otherwise."

"Has the temptation ever arisen?"

"Seventy-five percent of the events I organize are social events—parties, galas, weekend bonding trips. Alcohol-fueled testosterone tends to result in passes being made."

His hand tightened around his glass, his gaze turning hard as it rested on her. "Has it ever gone beyond making a pass?" he asked silkily.

"Just once. Luckily, my knee-to-crotch reflexes were razor sharp. By the time he sobered up, he'd forgotten the incident."

He relaxed a little. "So I stymied your chances at a promotion?"

"Sheena, my boss, had a hard-on for getting your business soon after the Indigo Lounge venture kicked off. She's been dying to expand the company for a while. We submitted a proposal, but it was very thin on the ground due to a lack of info."

"Most of my companies are listed on the stock market."

"Yes, but she wanted an extra edge."

He nodded. "Fair enough. I'd do the same in that situation."

"Yes, so I visited your New York offices and spoke to one of your press officers about Indigo. She revealed nothing beyond what was already in the public domain."

He grinned unapologetically.

"But she did tell me about the extra guests you allowed on your planes. I told Keely—"

"Your sexed-up friend," he inserted dryly.

Bethany laughed. "Yep. She pushed me into signing up, and I guess the rest is history."

He shook his head. "Not history. We're only just beginning, baby." He rose from his chair, discarding his glass with a casual grace that had her insides clenching with impossible lust. He caught her up and brought her close to his body. She was totally unsurprised to find that his erection hadn't subsided. One hand gripped her hair, exposing her jaw and neck to his soft kisses, as the other clamped around her waist. "What's Keely's last name?"

"Why?" she asked after forcing breath into her lungs.

"Because I owe her big for her role in bringing you into my life." His tongue rimmed her lips. The action had the immediate and damning effect of liquidizing her insides and wetting her sex.

"Even though you suspected I had an ulterior motive just now?"

He pulled back slightly and gazed down at her. "I don't apologize for double-checking my place in your life, Bethany. A man in my position has to learn to question any and all angles. Besides, I don't trust easily."

"I know. I recall a very thorough frisking in your office."

One corner of his mouth lifted, but his face remained serious. "Only time will prove both our intentions. I hope you're okay with that?"

She hesitated. What he said did make sense, although an irrational part of her wanted his trust of her to be immediate and unquestioning. Deep down she knew she trusted him on some level, at least enough for her to have made the decision to abandon the Indigo Lounge trip to come to Paris with him.

But then, she'd trusted Chris implicitly. Until he'd dropped his bombshell in her lap.

Caution was good. Caution was essential.

"Yes. I'm okay with that."

He exhaled, and a look of relief crossed his face before he slid both hands over her ass and squeezed tight.

When she shuddered in response, he groaned, pulled her closer and lifted her up.

"Put your legs around me, baby."

She complied, bringing her damp center flush against his rock-hard erection. He started to walk back into the suite. Being this close to his warm, gorgeous body made desire burn hotter.

Unable to wait any longer, she caught his face between her hands and took his mouth in a hot, needy kiss.

He stumbled, and she heard his hand slap the glass door to steady himself. Chest heaving, he deepened the kiss, his tongue sliding against hers in an erotic promise of what his cock would do to her in the very near future.

Needing him more than she'd ever needed anything in her life, she rocked her hips against his rigid length.

"Shit. I can't think straight when you do that."

"Good, I don't want you thinking straight. It's only fair because I can't think straight either." She rubbed her breasts against his chest and was rewarded with another pithy curse.

"Hold on, Peaches. Please, just another minute."

She whimpered, and he squeezed her ass. She heard the door slide open and they stumbled into the living room. Expecting him to tumble her onto the sofa as he had earlier, she jerked in surprise when he continued walking.

"I don't have any condoms here."

She gave another pathetic whimper. It would take at least a couple minutes to get to his suite. That was two minutes too long.

"I want you now, Zach! Please... it hurts."

"I know, sweet baby. I'll make it better in a minute. I promise. Just hold on."

Her fingers dug into his shoulders as he increased his stride. Even before he'd fully entered the bedroom, he was ripping away her panties. Her dress followed as soon as he set her down. His hot gaze glided over her as his hand went to his belt and tugged it off.

The moment he was naked, he grabbed her and threw her on the bed. Before she could draw another breath, two fingers slid into her wet heat, sending her already heightened senses spiraling out of control.

"I've been dying to fuck this tight little cunt for the last hour," he murmured just before he closed his mouth over one hard nipple.

Head rolling back, she spread her thighs wider. "Then what are you waiting for?"

10

She woke alone in bed the next morning. Disoriented for a moment, she slowly relaxed against the pillows as recollection dawned and replayed in vivid Technicolor.

Less than twelve hours ago, she'd become Zachary Savage's lover.

In that time, she'd had more sex than she'd had the past year. He'd been relentless with his demands, fucking her in more positions than she knew existed.

But more than that, an excitement burned inside her that had nothing to do with sex and everything to do with the prospect of having a dynamic man like Zach in her life. The stomach-knotting anxiety, which she had felt all through the trip to Shanghai and on the way to Paris, had subsided a little.

Things were moving a little too fast for her, but the knowledge that Zach was just as caught up in this fever of need they'd discovered for each other helped to ease that anxiety.

She stretched on the bed, her breath catching when inner and outer muscles protested at the workout they'd received at her lover's hand.

Slate-colored sheets warmed beneath her hands as she drifted them over the space Zach had slept in. Turning her head, she closed her eyes and inhaled his scent. Her pulse ramped up immediately. The plan had been to join The Indigo Lounge trip to blow away the pain and misery of the last six months and to have fun, but this...

"This is insane," she muttered.

"Talking to yourself, Peaches?"

She jerked upright.

He stood at the foot of the bed, shirtless and dressed in sweatpants. The sight of his broad shoulders, sculpted, hairless chest and tight six-pack made her mouth water.

It was obvious Zachary Savage looked after himself. Suddenly she felt pleased about her own regimen of running ten miles three times a week.

His gaze dropped to her naked breasts, and he licked his lips. "Come and eat your breakfast before I give in to the urge to eat you instead." Despite the growing erection, he started to turn away.

Disappointment cut deeper than it should have. "Am I that easy to resist all of a sudden?"

His gaze drifted over her, and she caught the slight flare of his nostrils as he exhaled. "Don't tempt me or we'll never leave this room. There's been a development. I prefer you to know about it sooner rather than later."

With that cryptic remark, he exited as quietly as he'd entered.

And just like that, the anxiety was back.

Jumping out of bed, she quickly shrugged on the silk robe supplied by the hotel. A brush through her hair provided a little composure.

Barefooted, she entered the sunlit dining room to find him reading a paper.

On the table, delicate croissants and *pain au chocolate*, coffee, fruit and condiments were spread on crystal tableware and sterling silver china.

He lowered his paper, rose and came around to where she sat. The casual kiss he dropped on her head made her breath catch. Without speaking, he spread a linen napkin over her lap and poured her a coffee. Once he'd added the prerequisite spoon of sugar and a drop of cream, he set it down in front of her and returned to his seat.

His lips firmed as he picked up the spare newspaper and pushed it across the table. "Page seven."

Her heart lurched and she curled her fists in her lap. "What's on page seven?" she asked.

He remained silent but his eyes stayed on her as she slowly reached for the paper and opened it with trembling fingers.

A picture of Zach with a stunning, statuesque blonde, who had a hand on his shoulder and her face raised to his. She looked as if she was about to burst into tears.

Bethany recognized the heartbreak in her face. It was the same way she'd felt when Chris had dropped his bombshell and shattered dreams she'd nurtured for years.

She cast her gaze over the words. A few familiar words jumped out at her. Names too—Cindy, Isabelle, Farrah. But joined together, they meant nothing. She was cursing herself for not taking high school French seriously when he leaned closer.

"Zachary Savage Dumps Latest Flame."

He murmured the translation, but Zach may as well have shouted it. Because she was looking closer at the picture and seeing the clothes he wore yesterday when he'd left her for hours and hours. Just to confirm, she glanced at the date of the newspaper. The vice tightened harder around her chest.

She raised her gaze to his. "This was what you were doing yesterday?" Her voice shook almost as hard as her fingers. Irritated with herself for that humiliating show of emotion, she slammed the newspaper down. Unable to sit still any longer, she pushed her chair back and hurried away from the table. "Fuck you, Savage!" she threw over her shoulder.

"Bethany, wait!"

She heard his chair scrape across the terrace floor and broke into a run. It was insane how much she hurt. Insane and frightening.

He caught up with her just as she entered the hallway that led to their suite.

A hand on her arm stopped her. When she struggled against his hold, he pinned her to the wall, his hard thighs bracketing hers. "Baby, listen to me."

"Why should I? You left me here, cooling my heels so you could go dump your old girlfriend and come back and fuck your new one. It's not exactly axe murder territory but it ranks up there next to sleazebag. Jesus, do you know how that makes me feel?"

She tried to pull away. He held her tighter.

"That wasn't all I did yesterday—"

"God, please tell me you didn't fuck her goodbye." The very idea of it made her stomach flip over.

His jaw tightened. "Of course I didn't! Until last night, I hadn't fucked another woman in months."

The answer appeased her a little, but the knowledge of what he'd been doing was still wedged like stone beneath her breast, terrifying the living daylights out of her. How had this man come to mean so much to her in so short a time?

"Why did you show that picture to me? You could've kept it to yourself."

"Last night you told me you didn't like secrets. I can't share all of my life with you, but what I can I will make as transparent to you as possible."

"So you intend to tell me about every woman you've slept with since your balls dropped?"

His gaze hardened. "Don't get snippy, Peaches. Or I'll have to spank your gorgeous ass. I only told you about Sadie because you were already in my life before I'd made it clear she was out of mine. But I assure you it wasn't news to her."

A sudden thought struck her. "That's what you meant by 'when the time is right'!"

He nodded.

"It was also why you didn't touch me after that time in your office." His iron-strong restraint, his desperately hungry looks. It all made sense now.

"I didn't think it was right to lay a full claim on you when another woman felt she had the right to claim me. I wanted to finish things properly with her first."

She shook her head. "It still doesn't feel right..."

"Bethany, I've belonged to you since the moment I saw you. I had to make sure someone else knew that. That's all."

That floored her. In these days of dumping-by-text where guys felt perfectly absolved of any responsibility once they'd pressed send, Zach had flown thousands of miles to put things right with one girlfriend before starting with another. She'd seen the strain and naked hunger in his eyes from the moment they'd met. He'd stopped himself from acting on it until he was truly free.

But would the same thing happen to her when he met someone else? Would she also receive a visit from Zachary, informing her he now belonged to another woman? There was integrity in his action but also a cold bloodedness that struck a vein of terror in her heart.

"Don't overthink this, Bethany. My confrontation with Sadie was a long overdue thing. I'm sorry I had to do it after I met you rather than before, but once you came into my life, there was no question that it had to be done. Do you get that?"

"I'm trying to... but..." Her brain whirled with a flood of thoughts, but the most disturbing idea was that he'd been with another woman, one who'd known him intimately. That reality made her gut knot with acrid jealousy.

"What are you thinking, Peaches?" he murmured, drawing his hot body closer as if sensing her weakening. The hands that had been clamped on her waist now braced the wall on either side of her head, making her feel truly caged in, surrounded by him.

When his ripped torso leaned in closer, she fought to remember what her answer was.

"I'm thinking she didn't look like she was expecting the news you delivered yesterday..."

Beautifully sexy lips firmed. "I can't help that. Once I saw you, there was no prolonging this. The two days I had to wait to have you were the longest of my life," he growled in that sexy baritone that shivered all the way to her toes.

"I'm also thinking I'm not sure whether I want you more for displaying such nobility, or whether to claw your eyes out for leaving me here while you went to dump your old girlfriend."

He caught a swathe of hair in his fingers and brought it to his lips. Watching the mouth she was dying to devour work its way over her hair was so curiously erotic, she could only stare.

"I would much prefer it if you wanted me more." His mouth

dropped to graze along her jaw, sending a thousand sparks of desire racing across her nerve endings.

"I think that's near impossible right now." Not with that mouth moving so close to hers. Not when she could sense the barely leashed sexual predator prowling close, intent on consuming her.

His soft laugh tickled her earlobe. "But you can try harder."

"Maybe. Wait." She pushed at his shoulders until he leaned back from her. "You said that wasn't all you did. So where were you for the rest of the time?"

"I attended a three-hour meeting and finalized the deal I'd been working on."

"Oh, right." She made a quick calculation. "But that still doesn't make up for how long you were away."

He let loose that hot smile again. "You were counting the hours?"

"Answer the question, Zach." She didn't want to be that girlfriend who needed to know where her man was at every moment, but Zach had thrown the door wide open on this one. Besides, after being blindsided by Chris, her trust had taken a deep-sea diving excursion for the foreseeable future.

"No, I wasn't just at the meeting."

She looked into his eyes, saw the expectancy. "There's more, isn't there?"

"Clever girl. I was hoping you'd ask me that."

"Really? Why?"

She held her breath as he reached into his back pocket and withdrew a sheet of paper.

"Because I also stopped at my doctor's."

She jerked back so fast her head slammed against the wall.

He frowned. "Hey, watch it." He cradled the back of her head and rubbed gently where she'd banged it.

"Your doctor's? Why? Are you sick?" She couldn't disguise the slight panic in her voice. God, what was wrong with her? Three days ago, this man had been an enigma on a piece of paper, as far out of her reach as the stars were to humanity. Now all of a sudden, the thought that he could be suffering made her heart lurch alarmingly.

"No, I'm not sick. I can confirm that with one hundred percent certainty because I went to get some blood work done." His grey eyes held an extreme intensity, much more than usual, that made her heart skip several beats.

"Why would you need blood work done?"

"Because, while I don't mind using condoms and will continue to do so if you wish, I wanted to prove to you that I was healthy. Even before we touched, I knew you had the power to shred my control with the minimum of effort, Peaches."

She sucked in a breath. "I... do?"

"Yes. And that message has been confirmed a hundred-fold since we fucked. Are you on birth control?" he asked.

She nodded. "Quarterly shots to regulate my period. My latest dose was three weeks ago."

His gaze darkened and his mouth curved in a wicked smile. "Good." He thrust the paper into her hand. "This is for you."

With him this close, it took several minutes for her to read the health report. Zach was clean, a healthy, rampantly sexy male.

"You did this for me?"

"For us. I needed you to know that if I ever slip up and don't use protection, you'll never have to fear for your health. And also that we can indulge whenever we want without fearing any repercussions."

The paper fluttered from her hand and landed on the floor, unheeded. "So you mean... we can... I can..." She licked her lips, unable to convey the depth of emotions coursing through her at the images, which bombarded her brain.

He caught her to him with a jerky, needy movement, as if having her so far away physically hurt him. His hands curved over her ass, pulled her into sharp contact with his body. His cock was hard. Dear Lord, when wasn't his cock hard for her?

The knowledge sent yet another potent rush of powerful arousal through her. The idea that she, the woman whose boyfriend had dumped her for another man, could affect a guy as hot and sexually on top of his game as Zach, thrilled her and infused her with much needed confidence.

Leaning down, he bit on her earlobe. "It means you can have me whenever and wherever you want. Instant satisfaction. We don't have to wait. All you have to do when the mood takes you is to hop on and ride."

He laughed at the full-bodied shudder that went through her, and bit harder.

"Zach!"

He soothed the bite with his tongue. "Does that notion please you? Does it turn you on? Because that's what I want. You, turned on for me, twenty-four seven. The idea of that blows my mind, baby. Does it blow yours?"

"You know it does."

"Good. I'm glad." He pulled back slightly and glanced down at her, his eyelids heavy with a dangerously erotic look. "Hey, I believe we've just had our first fight."

"Hmm... I believe we have."

"So can we now progress to the making up sex?" He grinned.

Her breath hitched. "Right here?"

He caught her hand from around his waist and placed it on his cock. Her fingers curled around him. His groan was immediate and so heartfelt, she grew even wetter.

"This is as good a time as any, Peaches. I'm dying for you. I crave you the moment I walk out of your presence. Imagining your tight little cunt wrapped around my dick can only keep me going up to a point. Then things start to unravel for me."

Even as her insides melted at the thought of having him, hot and thick inside her, a part of her still dwelled on their conversation.

"Was she... Sadie... was she devastated that you ended things with her?"

Zach hesitated for a moment. "Yes, but it was the right thing to do. It was the only way I'd allow myself to be with you."

As someone who'd been dumped in favor of another, she felt a twinge of pain for the other woman. Getting dumped was most definitely not fun.

Impatient, his mouth started to descend again. She stopped him with a hand on his chest. "One more thing."

He growled. "Jesus, my fucking balls are on fire and you want to keep talking. Fine. One last question. That's all you get."

"Do you do this with all your girlfriends? The medical report thing?" she blurted before she could chicken out.

He froze, then blinked slowly. "No. You're the first one I've wanted to do it with. It never even occurred to me to do it with anyone else."

Her shocked exhalation made him smile. "Really?"

"Really. Do I get brownie points for that, baby?"

"Like you have no idea."

"Oh, one more thing you need to know, Peaches."

She loved that nickname, more than she would ever admit to him. "Yes?"

"From here on in, panties are banned. I want nothing to come between me and that fine, sexy ass of yours."

"Is that an order or a request?"

"It's whatever you need to convince yourself it is to make that reality happen. Disobey me and there will be consequences."

She knew he was being playful, but she couldn't stop the shiver of delight that went through her at his masterful tone.

"What do I get in return?"

"You can name when and where next time."

"That's it? I get to choose the place where you have your way with me?"

"Yes. It's a great deal. You should take it."

With deft hands, he pulled the robe free of her body and stared down at her for so long and so hard, her nipples ached and her sex clenched and unclenched with needy pulls.

Strong, blunt-tipped fingers cupped her breasts and squeezed. "You're so beautiful, Peaches." Lowering his head, he feasted on her breasts until her fingers clawed desperately through his hair.

He took a condom out of his back pocket and tore it open with his teeth.

Surprise made her eyes widen. "But… I thought…"

Taking a step back, he yanked his joggers off and stepped out of them. Gloriously naked, heavily aroused, he hesitated, his eyes hopeful and eager in a way that made her sway towards him.

"Nothing would please me more, Bethany. But you get to say when that happens, okay?" he rasped.

She nodded. She'd never taken such a risk before, never even contemplated it with Chris. And yet here she was, almost on the verge of… of…

He reached out and cupped one cheek in his large palm. "It's okay to say no if you're not ready."

"I'm not ready."

His eyes dimmed a touch, but he nodded and held out the condom.

She took it from him and slid it on with sure, sexy strokes.

He stepped forward, and his cock nudged her entrance. "Take as long as you need, I can wait. As long as you're not fighting me or holding me back from this, I can wait. Jesus, I'm just grateful I get to have you any way I can get you. Are you ready for me?" One finger brushed past her clit and speared her tight sheath. Then it was swiftly joined by another. He fucked her with his fingers until stars danced behind her lids.

Desperate for more, she clawed at his shoulders. "Now, Zach. I'm ready. Please..."

With a hungry grunt, he kicked her legs wider apart and positioned the thick head of his cock at her entrance.

At the first thrust, she screamed.

Rough hands bit into her hips as he held her still for his penetration. She didn't last long.

Within a minute, she was unraveling. "Oh God! Oh—"

"Shit! Oh baby, I love the way you squeeze me when you come. Fuck, yeah. Just like that. Just like... ah!"

He buried his face in her throat and let out a loud keen as he pumped inside her.

Bethany held on as his release prolonged hers.

When the thought danced in her head, she let it sink in. Just how would it feel to take Zach Savage skin to skin?

11

"Bethany, thank God! What the fuck is going on?" Keely screamed in her ear the moment she answered the phone.

"Why? What's happened?" Bethany's eyes darted to where Zach sat next to her, his fingers swirling dangerously up her thigh. Even through the fabric of the white Capri pants she wore, his touch electrified her.

There were several other seats on the plane, but he'd chosen the seat right next to her. And of course he knew his proximity was playing havoc with her thinking abilities because he was wearing a smug, sexy smile.

"I had a case of vintage Dom Perignon and the most gorgeous purple calla lilies delivered to my apartment this morning," Keely all but yelled.

"And that's bad, why?"

"It was signed, 'Thanks for my Peaches.' I have no idea where they came from or who the fuck Peaches is. But it was signed with a Z... so...?"

Bethany's eyes widened at Zach, and his smile grew when

she mouthed, *WTF?* When her gaze promised hell, he answered by moving his fingers higher until they grazed her mound.

The lack of panties made his touch extra sensitive. Her breath caught, and she bit her lip hard to stop from groaning. He'd just taken her, with a condom, in his luxury bedroom at the back of the plane barely half an hour ago, and yet she burned for him more intensely than ever. The depth of the consuming need was terrifying her, hence her need to connect with Keely. Her best friend brought a refreshing dose of sanity, which she'd felt slipping from her ever since she'd clapped eyes on Zach Savage.

"Hey, you there?"

"Yes, Keel, I'm here, but I'm on a plane, so I don't know how good the connection is—"

"The connection is perfect," Zach volunteered loud enough for Keely to hear.

"Right... Can someone with a good command of English please tell me what's going on?" Keely demanded, her voice crackling with impatience.

Zach calmly held out his free hand for the phone. Bethany raised a brow and pursed her mouth. He retaliated by pressing his fingers harder between her legs. She quickly relinquished the phone.

He tapped the speaker button and propped the phone on his knee. "Keely, it's Zachary Savage."

"Hey."

Zach's mouth did that one-side tilt thing that made her clit throb. "I wanted to show my appreciation in getting Bethany to sign up for The Indigo Lounge tour and for getting her to Newark on Sunday. I understand you had a big role to play in that."

"Yep, it was all me," Keely replied smugly.

"I hope you like the champagne and flowers."

"A case of vintage Oenothèque champagne worth ten thousand dollars? What's not to like? But what's with the Peaches?"

He turned his head and watched her, still with that smile. "Do you mind if I don't divulge that?" His eyes raked slowly over Bethany. When they reached where his fingers rested, they darkened a touch before they rose to meet hers again.

He was aroused. Deeply, erotically, hungrily aroused just by looking at her.

Bethany couldn't wrap her mind around that.

"Well, okay, sure. But promise me one thing?" her friend demanded.

Zach rasped, "I'll try."

"Whatever you do, don't fucking graduate to calling each other Honey Boo Boo. I don't want to puke into my Dom P."

"You're welcome, Keely."

She grunted. "You'll keep, Zachary Savage. Just look after my girl, or I'll come after you with a blunt instrument. Dom Perignon or no Dom Perignon."

His grey eyes danced with merriment. "Understood." He took the phone off speaker and passed it back to her.

"You're okay?" Bethany asked.

"As long as you are. I'm keeping Iron Balls updated with news of Aunt Mel. She's getting worse by the day."

Bethany laughed then sighed. "As long as you make sure my Aunt Mel makes a miraculous recovery before I come back, I'll let you run with it. Karma can be a bitch, and I'm not having my aunt's life toyed with."

"Don't worry, I told you I've got your back. Umm, am I still on speaker?"

Her gaze flickered to Zach. He'd leaned his head against the headrest but his eyes were still trained on her. "No," she said.

"So everything okay with you? Is he treating you well? Are you having fun?"

"Yes, yes and yes."

"Great. Keep it that way. And keep in touch, for God's sake. You know how much I hate to be left hanging."

"I will. Bye, Keely. Love you."

She rang off. Zach continued to watch her. "What?"

"I like her."

She paused to consider if his words were meant to be superficial or not, then berated herself for trying to read too much into the situation. "Good. She's important to me."

His gaze turned speculative. "How important?"

"Are there categories of important?"

He shrugged. "I just want to know if I have to compete with her for your attention once we return to the real world."

About to answer in the negative, she paused. "She's been there for me every time I've needed her."

His gaze bore into hers. "And how badly have you needed her?"

"Very badly six months ago. And a lot since then. She's been my rock." Despite her effort to not sound shaky, he heard the slight tremble in her voice. His nostrils flared slightly, a sign that she'd come to recognize meant he was seriously pissed about something.

"Tell me what that asshole did to you."

"Who, Chris?" She shrugged, but the burn of humiliation seared her insides. "He decided he preferred other assholes. Literally. And of the male persuasion."

Zach's eyes widened. Then his jaw tightened. The hand on her mound slid lower, gripped her harder, possessively. That hold centered her, made her think of no one else, nothing else but him.

"He told you he preferred men?"

"He didn't just tell me. He called me after work one Friday night and asked me to meet him. I thought we were going for our regular drinks and dinner. Instead he introduced me to his gay lover at a bar we frequented. Then said gay lover came with him to the apartment we shared and helped him pack his belongings. Turns out they'd been apartment-hunting for a few weeks—weeks I thought he was away for work. They'd decided they wanted to make it official once they'd found a place to live. They're living together in a loft in Soho."

"Fuck." He cupped her nape and lifted her into his lap. Once he'd settled her comfortably, his hand returned to its position between her thighs. "You know what he is?" he grated out.

The tears tightening her throat made it hard to speak. She shook her head.

"He's a coward and an asshole. Any guy who needs moral support to break things off doesn't deserve you. And any guy who can't see what a priceless treasure you are didn't deserve to have you in the first place."

The rush of tears surprised the hell out of her when it really shouldn't have. She was going through a whole new level of experiences with Zach. Experiences that she knew would shock the hell out of her before this thing was over.

Blinking back the tears clouding her vision, she tried to laugh but only managed a croaky cough. "You're earning yourself serious brownie points right now."

He grimaced. "I'll take them. But I don't need them to tell you how beautiful you are. How utterly gorgeous and sexy and generous and warm-hearted. How endlessly mesmerizing. He couldn't see that, so it's his loss."

This time, she couldn't stop the flood. Cursing, he brushed them away with his thumb.

"Don't cry, baby. Not for a dickhead like that."

"I'm not crying for him. I'm crying because... because..." She shook her head. "Thank you."

"For stating the truth? For wanting you to see that you deserve to be worshipped? I intend to tell you that often and consistently. Until you believe it."

"You make me want to believe it. When you touch me, I feel beautiful."

"That's because you are. Every. Single. Inch. Of you. Every time I'm with you, I want to show you how beautiful you are. Hell, Peaches, I walk around with my dick hard enough to hammer nails. I'm surprised there's enough blood left in my brain to be able to put one foot in front of the other."

She laughed, and the intensity in his eyes eased, but not the hunger. The hunger was always there. And the fact that it was aimed at her turned her on so hard she trembled.

"You're getting that look again," he mused.

"What look?"

"That glazed look that tells me you're thinking naughty thoughts." His hand slipped from her nape and into her hair, caressing her scalp before fisting his fingers in a possessive hold.

"Can you blame me? I can feel your thick, beautiful cock underneath my ass. You're saying beautiful things to me. Between your mouth and your cock, I'm hopelessly lost and shamelessly addicted. I want you so much, Zach. So very badly."

He groaned and rested his forehead against hers. "I want you, too. But as much as I want to do something precise and pleasurable about it right now, we can't. We're landing in less than ten minutes."

She jerked upright. "Really?"

Craning her neck, she looked out of the nearest window. All

she could see was arid, hauntingly beautiful desert interspersed with isolated clumps of greenery.

"Yep. And don't look so disappointed. I intend to satisfy every single craving you've ever had." He returned her to her seat, leaned across and secured her seatbelt. "Now repeat after me. Often and thoroughly."

"Often and thoroughly."

He smiled. "Good girl."

* * *

Zach watched Bethany closely as she got her first glimpse of Marrakech. It wasn't for everybody. Certainly, when he'd brought Sadie here, she'd complained long and loudly about the humidity and the heat.

Whereas he didn't mind. Growing up in Louisiana had meant long sultry summers. And while he had wished himself away from his birthplace long before he escaped, there was something about heat that he'd found deeply arousing and almost spiritual.

The summers he'd spent with his mother, when she'd been lucid enough to function, had been special.

Pain sliced through him, but he pushed it away and concentrated on the woman next to him.

The woman whom he was beginning to suspect could burrow under his skin if he let down his guard. The woman he couldn't get nearly enough of no matter how much they fucked.

And boy, did he love fucking her.

"Where are we now?" she asked as their air-conditioned, partitioned jeep drove through streets teeming with jellebah-clad locals and eager tourists.

"We're passing through the Old Town. Over there is the Medina, the historical district."

Her head whipped toward where he pointed, her eyes wide with pleasure.

"You like it?"

She smiled. "I love what I've seen so far. How far to your place?"

He nodded towards the snow-capped Atlas Mountains, which soared in the distance. "Half an hour away. The chopper would've been quicker, but I wanted you to see the city up close."

"Why Marrakech?"

Zach hesitated, ingrained self-preservation triggers kicking in. The thought that perhaps Marrakech wasn't the right destination choice fleeted through his mind. When her smile began to dim, he gritted his teeth. "I backpacked through Africa six years ago. Morocco was one of my stops. It grew on me, so I bought a place down here."

Her face brightened again, and he realized he'd been holding his breath. He released it and moved closer to her. It certainly had nothing to do with the fact that he floundered every time he revealed a little bit more of himself. With Bethany, he felt obliged to share parts of himself he'd never revealed to anyone, not because he wanted to, but because he saw how much it meant to her.

"I can't imagine you backpacking."

His smile felt tight. The backpacking in itself was no big deal. It was the reason behind it that he didn't want to reveal. "Well, I did. All the way, even down to the flip-flops."

"Hmmm, flip-flops... sexy." She swayed toward him. He closed the distance and rubbed his thumb over her lips. When her vivid blue eyes darkened, he groaned and pulled back.

"We need to watch it. I won't be able to control myself once I start kissing you." He couldn't indulge his need for her right now, but the jeep's windows were tinted enough that he could slide his hand down her thighs to rest it between her legs, in that place where he most desired to be.

When she jerked against his touch, he grew harder. God, he'd couldn't remember when he'd been this hard this constantly. If he didn't love fucking her so much it would be a damn inconvenience.

"Maybe we should've taken the chopper after all," she murmured, her gaze on the very telling evidence of his excitement beneath his jeans.

"Trust me, Peaches, I won't make that mistake again." Grabbing her hand, he placed it over his erection then groaned again when the pain threatened to eviscerate him.

Out of sight of Philip, who was behind the wheel, he pressed her hand harder onto his straining hard-on and worked her palm up and down.

He watched her face, watched her excitement grow as he grew thicker in her grasp. When her tongue circled her lips, he bit back a filthy curse. He caught her nape and dragged her close.

"Stop doing that," he warned in her ear.

"Zach, you've trapped my hand under yours," she whispered back fiercely.

"I don't mean that. I mean what you're doing with your tongue. It makes me think you want to suck my cock all the way to the back of your throat and thoroughly enjoy doing it."

Her free hand clamped hard on his thigh. "What if I want to do just that?" she responded boldly. "You have an exceptionally beautiful cock."

"Then I say you'll get your chance sooner rather than later."

He pulled away and pressed the intercom that connected to

the front. "We're done with the scenic route, Philip. Get us to the house asap." He sat back and watched a delicate wave of heat wash over her face. "Now's not the time to be coy, Peaches. You've stated a wish, and it's my duty to fulfill it."

She laughed, a husky sound that triggered a pleasurable hum inside him. "You're about to get a blow job, and you're making it sound like you're doing me a favor?"

"I intend to make it a pleasurable experience for both of us. And never doubt it, baby, I'll take care of you before we're done."

He watched her swallow and take a deep breath. He tried a few of those himself and felt marginally more in control of his violent hunger.

"How long before we get there?" The strain in her voice mirrored how he felt.

"Ten minutes."

"Okay, I need a distraction. So you sent Keely champagne and flowers. Care to discuss?"

"There's nothing to discuss. I meant what I said. I wanted to show her my appreciation."

"But you don't know her from Eve. What makes you think she wouldn't have run to the nearest tabloid to sell her story once she knew you sent her the present?"

"I trusted that you wouldn't be friends with someone like that."

She sucked in a breath as her stunning eyes connected with his. "I... Thank you."

"You're welcome." He refrained from telling her he'd had Keely quietly vetted. He didn't regret taking the precaution. He'd been too badly burned in the past to take risks on faith anymore.

But he trusted Bethany. Something about her made him want to let go of his rigid trust issues.

"You're still looking at me as if I have an ulterior motive," he said.

"It's not that. I guess I'm a little puzzled. When I searched for you on the internet, I found next to nothing about you personally. And yet, here you are, three days after meeting me, putting yourself out in public with little care for the risks involved."

"Some risks are worth taking."

Her eyes widened. "And I'm one of them?"

He nodded. "I've only known you for three days, nevertheless I've taken risks with you that I've never taken with anyone else. I could get seriously burned here, but I'm willing to take the step."

"Zach... I don't know what to say."

"You don't need to say anything. Just keep giving me what you're giving me—your companionship and that gorgeous body."

"You have it." She breathed out her response with such fervor that he felt lightheaded.

Jesus. She was so amazing. So giving. The hunger, which had almost consumed him when he'd first set eyes on her, intensified. At this rate, he'd be on his knees day and night for her if he wasn't careful.

With relief, he saw Philip turn onto the long private dirt road that led to his place. Of all his homes, this was the one he was most proud of. He couldn't wait to show it off to Bethany. Right after he'd fucked her. And came in her mouth. And fucked her some more.

His hand tightened on her nape. She jerked but didn't pull away. He liked that. Loved the fact that she wasn't scared of how demanding he could be. She wasn't scared of his hunger for her.

It would make the next several days all the more enjoyable, knowing that he didn't have to hold back.

Even more so once he'd shown her the delights of his toy room.

* * *

Zach's place was more like a palace.

It was stunning. There was only one drawback.

Water flowed everywhere.

The old fear slammed into Bethany with the force of a hurricane and kept slamming into her when, with each room they passed, all she saw was a view of the various water features outside.

Zach was too intent on reaching his destination—his bedroom, she suspected—to notice her tension. Bethany was glad of that because it was one way of combatting the fear and anxiety rushing through her.

Rich tapestries and gleaming marble floors whizzed by as they almost jogged through rooms filled with history and beauty.

His suite, once they reached it, was equally breathtaking. The raised bed, one of the largest she'd ever seen, made a bold statement that set her pulse racing.

Beyond the wide muslin-curtained windows, the sound of a fountain tinkled.

Inside, the tension in the air grew as Zach tracked her to where she dropped her purse and kicked off her shoes. His chest heaved as he took deep breaths.

Taking her time, she plucked her Oliver Peoples sunglasses off her head and placed them on the tallboy nearby.

Then she took off her Capri pants and the dark gold linen and lace sleeveless top.

Cool air from discreet air-conditioners washed over her

heated skin, causing goosebumps of anticipation. She stood only in the indigo bra she'd bought in Paris and changed into after their sex session on the plane.

Zach's gaze took in the color, dropped to her panty-less crotch, and his breath hissed out. "You're wearing my favorite color."

"Do you like it?"

He started unbuttoning his shirt. "Come over here and I'll let you know."

Before she'd taken a step, he was shrugging off his white shirt. The sight of his glorious torso made her insides melt and her mouth water. He was so gorgeous. His face was a work of art, and his body made hers sing in worship. She still had a hard time believing he was truly into her.

She reached him and stopped. As he worked his jeans button free and lowered his zipper, he continued to watch her.

"What do you want to do, Peaches?" he rasped.

She wet her lower lip. "I want your cock in my mouth."

He closed his eyes for a few control-gathering seconds as he pushed his jeans off and kicked them away. When she stepped closer and grasped his waist, his eyes flew open.

Keeping hers on him, she slowly sank to her knees.

He groaned long and rough. "God, seeing you on your knees makes me so fucking hard."

Her fingers whispered over the erection tenting his boxers, and she smiled. "You're already hard, Zach."

"Harder then. So much harder. I feel as if I'm about to explode, baby." Fervid fingers freed her loosely held hair from its clasp.

"Not just yet. I want to taste you for a little while." She ran her hands up his thighs, felt the warm, corded muscle beneath her touch.

"Fuck, yes." He cradled the back of her skull in an urgent caress. "I need you so much, baby." His face was a stark mask of raw desire.

She cupped his balls and felt them tightened in her palm. "I need you too."

Wetting her lips some more, she took his wide head in her mouth. He jerked against her and cursed.

She played her tongue over the ridged edge and felt the blood surge under the velvety skin.

"Christ!"

Having learned very quickly that Zach didn't like losing control for very long, Bethany decided to move fast. She swirled her tongue over him and took his cock as far into her mouth as she could. He filled her, his thick veins pulsing with power and vitality as she sucked him.

She smiled in feminine pride as he groaned his appreciation. "Oh, Peaches, you're so very good at that." As she'd known he would, he soon took over. With both hands cupping the back of her head, Zach rocked his cock in her mouth, establishing a rhythm that had him hitting the back of her throat over and over again.

The hotness of it was so decadent, so beautifully filthy, liquid heat dampened her sex and her clit swelled.

"Look at me, Bethany." She tilted her head and stared into heavy-lidded, aroused eyes. "You love having me at your mercy, don't you? Love seeing me this undone?"

"Hmm." Her hummed answer made him jerk harder as her vibrating glands hit his sensitive head.

"God, you're going to make me come!"

"Hmmm," she tried again.

His thighs shook and his balls contracted. The first gush of semen made her almost gag. She struggled to swallow as much of his warm, salty taste as she could.

He drew back.

She gulped in air and grasped the root of his cock. "More," she demanded.

"Jesus! How fucking greedy are you?" He slammed back in and stayed there, spurting harder into her mouth. Deep shudders shook him from head to toe as he emptied himself completely.

Bethany couldn't get enough. Hollowing her cheeks, she sucked every last drop until he pulled out with a pained grimace. He was still semi-hard. Zach never went completely soft. It was almost as if he was primed at all times to fulfill her every need.

"Baby, I think you've sucked me dry." Tilting her chin, he took her mouth in a hot kiss before he lifted her up off the floor. "I think it's only fair I reciprocate."

He tossed her onto his bed then watched with hungry eyes as she wiggled on her back to the middle. "Take off your bra. It's so pretty, and I don't want to ruin it."

With shaky hands, she unclipped her bra and threw it at him. He caught it with his teeth and pretended to maul it. Laughing despite the desire snaking through her belly, she settled deeper into the mattress.

He flung the bra away and prowled onto the bed. Nuzzling the crook of her neck, he inhaled deeply. "You smell so good. And I bet you're soaking wet, too. Did you get that way from sucking me off, Peaches?"

"Yes," she said breathily.

Grabbing a pillow, he placed it next to her hip. "Turn over and lie on the pillow for me." He waited until she complied. "Now I want you to spread your legs. As wide as you can."

Heart pumping loud enough to deafen her, Bethany spread her legs. But he wasn't satisfied.

"Come on, baby. You can do better than that," he encouraged.

She stretched wider, until her legs were almost perpendicular to her body, and her sex was wide open to his scorching gaze.

Bethany flushed with embarrassment and acute anticipation. She was unbelievably wet from having him at her mercy, from feeling his life force pump down her throat. She'd never felt more exposed. Or more excited.

Zach made a sound of approval in his throat and positioned himself between her legs. His hands slid over her ass and slapped both globes. She gasped as the sting of pain mingled with her excitement to make her even wetter. He slapped her again, then groaned.

"So pink. So gorgeous. So very wet for me. You're unbelievable, you know that?"

She whimpered, the need to have his mouth right there a cloying necessity consuming her from the inside.

"Zach, please!"

"Soon, baby. Right now I just want to look at you."

"Do it, please. God, please do it." She clawed her hair to one side and turned to watch him. The acute hunger on his face almost stopped her breath. But she'd come to learn that he wouldn't give in to it until he was good and ready.

Frustrated, she started to turn. A sharp slap on her ass had her holding still. "That's not fair, Zach!"

"Oh, but it is. You had me at your mercy just now. I wasn't ready to come, but you worked me with that wicked tongue and that gorgeous mouth of yours. I blew my load long before I was ready. Now, it's your turn to suffer."

He lowered his head and blew a hot breath on her clit. He

held her down as she jerked, then he blew again and grazed his teeth over her nerve-filled nub.

"Oh!"

"More?"

"Yes!"

He flicked his tongue several times and then pulled her clit into his mouth, then proceeded to suck on it like it was his favorite candy.

Brutal pleasure screamed through her. Stars danced behind her clamped eyelids. Tension screamed through her thighs as her sex clenched around his probing tongue.

"So fucking greedy," he crooned.

He stabbed his tongue deeper. Bethany bit down hard on the pillow to stop her from begging him to finish her off. Sliding his fingers through her wet slit, he worked his way to her other tight opening. At the first touch of his thumb pressing down, a different sort of pleasure ploughed through her.

The triple sensation of finger, tongue and mouth pushed her over the edge. She gushed into his mouth, screaming her climax. Shudders rolled over her as he drank her in, his tongue lapping her, over and over, as he swallowed every creamy drop.

Caressing his body over hers, he rested on his elbows and nuzzled his cheek against hers. "Feel good?"

"Hmmm. Better than good." She felt limp, floating on a sea of sheer bliss. Somehow, she found the strength to lower her legs, grateful when he didn't protest.

Of course, she found out a second later that he had other plans when he flipped her over and positioned his cock at her entrance.

As she gazed up into his gorgeous face, renewed excitement slammed inside her. The ravenous hunger was still there. When he kissed her with bruising intensity, she tasted her juices on his lips. The mouth that had devoured her sex moments ago now devoured her mouth. Then he was trailing hot kisses all over her face, along her jaw to her earlobe.

"Condom or no?" he rasped in her ear.

Although she'd known this moment would come, Bethany froze at the question. She was stepping into totally unknown territory here. And not just physically. This was a first for both of them. Once she took this step, there would be no going back.

But she'd already strayed further out of her comfort zone than she'd ever done before. The moment she'd set eyes on Zachary Savage, she'd been lost. He was like no other man she'd ever met.

And when he said he would protect her, she believed him.

She looked into his eyes. "I want to feel your skin against mine. Inside me."

His eyes darkened and his breath punched from his chest. "Peaches," he breathed.

One hand slid beneath her nape, and the other caught her knee and curved it over his hip.

Slowly, he slid into her, inch by delicious inch. The sensation was glorious, raw and earthy. Her tissues, swollen by the force of her earlier orgasm, stretched as he pushed deeper inside her. The head of his cock touched the edge of her womb, brushed that secret place which made her whole body tingle with super-sensitive delight.

"Zach..."

"I know, baby. I feel it too." Jaw gritted tight, he pulled back and glanced down her body to his cock, glistening with her slick juices. "God," he groaned. He slammed back inside her, his movements not as refined as before. A deep shudder rocked him from head to toe. She bit her lip with the profound knowledge that she was doing this to him.

Bethany stretched her legs wider to accommodate him, to accommodate the overwhelming sensation of being fucked raw for the first time in her life. When he lowered his head, she surged up to meet his kiss.

Her mouth fused to his, and clinging on to his shoulders for dear life, she met him thrust for thrust, sucking him greedily into her body each time. His groans escalated into prolonged moans as he fought for breath.

Ecstasy danced close, teasing her with its promise of the best climax of her life. The anticipation was almost as bad as the unraveling. "Oh, God… I can't… It's too much, Zach!"

He fisted her hair and held her still. "You can. Just a little bit longer, baby. It'll be worth it, I promise." He rocked his hips in a series of deep stabbing moves that had her gasping.

"It's worth it now. More than worth it. Please… I want to come so bad!" She tightened her thighs around his waist and squeezed, feeling the tell-tale euphoria steal over her.

"That's it, baby. Squeeze me with your sweet, tight cunt." He lowered his head and pulled one hard nipple into his mouth.

The sensation transmitted straight to the hunger between her legs, causing her muscles to spasm. She came long and hard, with a force that rocked her from head to toe.

"Fuck!" Zach groaned. "I'm going to come so hard for you, Peaches." His shouted release was the deepest she'd heard. Hot semen flooded inside her with such force that she feared she would drown from it. Endlessly he spurted, his gasps music to her ears as he shuddered helplessly in her arms.

The thought that this was his first time too sent a powerful sensation through her. She soothed a hand down his back until his shudders gentled into occasional spasms, and she didn't care one iota that his weight crushed her into the bed.

After endless minutes, he lifted his head. "I'm sorry, I know I'm crushing you, but I can't move." His body jerked again.

"I'm okay. Besides, I can't move either."

He laughed, then relaxed back into her arms. "Hey, Peaches?"

"Hmm?"

"You might want to consider getting full-body insurance. I can't promise that you won't be permanently bow-legged by the time I'm done with you."

"Ditto," she whispered in his ear.

His deep laugh resonated within her. "Let's hit the shower, then I'm giving you the grand tour."

12

"You have a ballroom?" Bethany gasped and moved deeper into the large circular room. Frescoes depicting turbaned sultans and voluptuous half-naked servants colored the walls and soared up the Moroccan ceilings. Beneath her feet, the marble floors gleamed with high polish, and she had no trouble imagining the room filled with beautiful people enjoying beautiful music, while sipping champagne and nibbling on canapés.

Unable to help herself, she twirled in a perfect pirouette, followed by a quick fist-pump in celebration that she hadn't forgotten how.

Zach was smiling when she turned to face him, his head tilted slightly as he watched her. "It came with the house. It serves as a perfect entertainment center when I'm this close to Europe."

"Wow. I seriously love it." They had passed the entrance to the room on their way to Zach's bedroom, but she hadn't had a chance to see it fully. She glanced around again. Then she self-consciously tucked her hair behind her ears when she realized how intently Zach watched her.

"Enough to do that pirouette thing for me again?" he asked with another devastating smile.

With an answering smile, she stepped back to give herself enough room. Then, raising herself on her toes, she performed the move for him again, and added a couple more just for good measure.

When she finished her last twirl, he caught her face in his hands and kissed her. "That was beautiful. Stay here. I have a present for you."

He left her standing in the middle of the room and walked to the far side, where a box she hadn't spotted when they entered the room stood. Striding back to her, he held out the large ribboned package to her.

The most glorious satin ballet slippers lay within luxury tissues. She caught sight of the specialized designer label and gasped. "Oh, my God, Zach. These cost thousands of dollars!"

He shrugged and dropped the empty box. "Money doesn't matter. Do you like them?"

"Are you kidding? I love them!" Stupid tears stung behind her lids. She forced them away and glanced up at him. "But I don't know when I'll ever use them."

"Have you given any thought to dancing again, just for your own pleasure?"

"Not really. But I suppose it's not out of the question." She stroked the slippers, the old yearning rising to the fore. "I've put on too much weight to even think about it."

"Bullshit. You're perfect. If it makes you happy, do it."

Tears stung harder, and her heart did that stupid little kick again. Suddenly, breathing became difficult as sensations, which had nothing to do with sex, pounded at her. She could fall for this guy so very easily.

"Besides, my motives weren't altogether altruistic."

She blinked. "Oh really?"

He shook his head, caught her around the waist and twirled her once before pulling her close. "Ever since you told me about your ballet training, I've dreamed of fucking you while you hold the arabesque position," he breathed into her mouth. He swallowed her gasp and let her come up for air a full minute later.

"I think I've fallen into the arms of a kinky freak."

He laughed. "You have no idea."

Taking the slippers from her, he placed them back in the box and set it down on the floor. He took her hand. After kissing her knuckles, he wove his own through them and led them from the room.

The hallway held the same elaborate frescoes but in a broader subject matter, leaning towards more Eastern influences. "These are stunning," she said.

"They were crumbling a little when I bought the house. Restoration took a while, but I'm glad I stuck with it."

"You keep calling it a house. I think the right term is palace. It's huge. Certainly more than big enough for one person."

He turned his face away from her. "I needed a private place. It suited my purpose."

He led her out onto a wraparound terrace that overlooked the mountains. The air was dry and humid and stung her lungs. But the combined scents of spices and clean air thrilled her sensory receptors. She took another breath, turned around and saw the enormous hot tub.

Frozen, she stared at it.

Zach glanced from her stricken face to the tub and back again. She heard him speak, but her attention was riveted to the sight in front of her.

"Bethany!"

She turned wide eyes to him.

"What is it?"

"I don't... I don't like water."

He frowned. "It's just a tub."

She shook her head. "Not to me," she blurted.

His frown intensified. "Do you want to leave?"

"No. I love this place."

"Aside from the water."

She tried for a shrug. "As long as you don't expect me to swim in the pool or take a bath with you, I think I'll be okay."

His eyes dimmed with disappointment, and he walked her back inside the house. The rest of the tour was conducted in a subdued manner. Each time they neared his pool or the fountain, he glanced anxiously at her.

Bethany knew she'd grown pale by the time they entered the bespoke kitchen. He led her to one of the large islands and pulled out a stool for her. Pouring a glass of mineral water, he set it in front of her.

"How long have you had a fear of water?"

She shrugged. "I don't remember when it started exactly. But I nearly drowned when I was younger. Twice. Once by accident. And the other time..."

His eyes narrowed. "Someone deliberately tried to drown you?"

She nodded.

"Who?" he breathed in that quietly dangerous way she'd come to denote as fury. She'd heard the same note in his voice when she'd talked about Chris.

The power behind it sent a shiver over her skin. As cowardly as it was, she wanted the atmosphere gone. "It doesn't matter, Zach. I don't want to talk about—"

"Who was it, Bethany?"

She passed a hand over her nape to soothe the anxiety

rushing through her. "Our neighbor's son. He was a little older than me and used to come over to swim in our pool when he was home from college. I was fourteen at the time and he... he used to watch me." She shrugged. "I kinda had a little crush on him. But I never thought..."

"He would return the crush?"

"Yes. Anyway, one day he tried to kiss me. Things got a little heavy. I tried to get him to stop. He got angry."

"And he tried to fucking drown you? Where were your parents?" His nostrils were pinched, and his eyes were a dark, furious grey.

"They were next door with his parents. It all happened so fast."

"It only takes seconds, Bethany." His eyes grew stormier. "Did you tell your parents?"

"No."

"Surely they must have wondered why you didn't swim anymore?"

She shrugged again. "I think they assumed my old fear had come back. It's not a big deal, Zach—"

"It is to me." Cradling her face in his large palms, he tilted her head and looked deep into her eyes. "You've suffered two near-death experiences and contended with that asshole of an ex too. It may not be much to you, but it's a fucking big deal to me. Tell me how to make it better," he said.

Her heart lurched. "Zach, you don't need to," she replied.

"I do. So many things could've kept you from me. I will take away all of your fears, Bethany. Each and every one of them. Or fucking die trying."

Her gasp made them both freeze. His eyes remained squarely on hers. Unwavering. Nonetheless, she felt him withdraw slightly, as if he'd also realized the emotive and shocking meaning of his words.

Abruptly, he dropped his hands. "Come on. We're almost done."

She followed him, sedate on the outside, raw and shaky on the inside. Lush plants, palm trees and luxury hammocks made up the elaborately designed garden.

But again, Zach's love of water was what caught her attention.

The pool extended from underneath the west side of the house and dissected the garden before dropping off in an infinity-style design almost a hundred meters away. Lined in slate grey, the bottom of the pool was almost indiscernible, escalating her nervousness.

Zach's fingers curled around hers, and he forced her to stop.

"The water isn't deep at this side. You don't need to come out here if you don't want to. The other side of the house has a garden without a pool. If you need to come out here for any reason, I'll be with you. If not, a member of my staff will always be with you."

She gave a jerky nod, and his fingers relaxed a touch.

He curled a hand over her nape and pulled her close. "Don't let the assholes win, Bethany. Just say the word and I'll help you put the bad memories to rest."

She pulled back and looked into his eyes. "Will you let me do the same for you?"

His eyes shadowed immediately, and he looked away, staring off towards the white peaks of the Atlas Mountains. "No need, baby. I have my demons well and truly covered."

"So you do have them?" she probed, her heart stalling then accelerating in anticipation of finding out a little bit more about this enigmatic man.

"Don't we all?"

"That's not really an answer, Zach. You're ready to cut down the people you think have wronged me, but you refuse to tell me even a little bit about what created those shadows in your eyes."

His frown made her pulse stutter, but she refused to look away or cower from it. "They don't impact us in any way, so they're irrelevant."

Again, she noted the evasive non-answer and curbed the frustration rising inside her. In the grand scheme of things, she was in danger of losing sight of the fact that she'd only known this man for three days.

Three. Short. Days.

It seemed as if a lifetime had passed, yet in all ways except carnal, they were virtual strangers.

Patience.

It wasn't a virtue she possessed in abundance, but she knew deep down that Zachary Savage wasn't a man you pushed.

Her stomach growled loudly, breaking the tension.

The smile that replaced his frown held a hint of relief. It was also blatantly calculated to fry her insides with its brilliance. "I guess our final destination is now determined." He tugged her after him as he rushed through the rest of the tour.

Twelve bedrooms, fifteen bathrooms, a golden-domed tower room accessed by interconnecting arches, and endless hallways later, they ended up back in the lavish kitchen.

Ordering her to sit at the high stool set into the center island, Zach strode to the giant fridge and started setting out ingredients on the counter.

"Can I do anything?" she asked, although secretly she wanted to do nothing more than sit and stare at the graceful movements of the man who succeeded in taking her breath away, even as he performed the most mundane of tasks.

"You can get us some wine." He indicated the deep alcove that held rack after rack of wines. "I'm making us a chicken couscous salad. Is that okay with you?"

She nodded as she slid off the stool and went to the wine chiller. She was by no means a wine connoisseur, but she guessed that anything she chose from Zach's selection would be a good choice. She grabbed the most familiar-looking label and returned to the island, fetching two glasses from the cabinet on her way.

Uncorking the wine, she poured and passed him a glass.

Eyes on hers, he took a long sip, set the glass down and moved the preparation to the center island. As he passed her, he stopped and dropped a kiss on top of her head.

He grabbed a large glazed earthenware pot and set it on the far side of the island.

"What's that?"

"It's a tagine pot." He lit the portable fire underneath it before he returned to the middle of the island where the chopping board was set.

Sunlight slanting through the large bay windows glinted off the knife and the short silky hairs on his wrist as he chopped vegetables and diced chicken. He tossed the chicken into the pot with herbs and a dash of oil then started on the salad.

"Where did you learn to cook?"

He shrugged. "Here and there. I picked up quite a bit on my travels, but I don't always get the chance to indulge." He looked up at her. "Forgive me if I'm a little bit rusty."

"You're talking to a girl whose other best friend is the local Italian takeout menu. You won't get any complaints from me." She took a sip of wine and told herself that watching him chop vegetables really wasn't as sexy as her jumpy hormones were trying to imply.

But she couldn't look away.

He moved to the tagine pot and raised the lid. The smell of sizzling, smoky chicken filled the air. Twenty minutes later, Zach served up their meal and took a seat next to hers.

Forking a mouthful of golden, herb-infused couscous and a bite of chicken, he held it out to her. "I need a verdict."

She took the mouthful and chewed. Rich textures exploded on her tongue, and she barely managed to stop from groaning in pleasure. Forcing herself to keep a straight face, she shrugged. "It's okay, I guess."

His eyes widened a touch before he frowned down at his plate. "What's wrong with it?"

"I'm not certain, exactly. Perhaps another bite to make sure?" she suggested.

Still frowning, he heaped another forkful and fed her. Again, she sampled the exquisite dish and shook her head. "I just don't know, Zach. I think you'll have to feed me the whole plate before I can make up my mind one way or the other."

"I have to..." He caught the quiver of laughter moving her shoulders and dropped the fork onto her plate.

"Gotcha," she crowed.

He grabbed either side of her stool and swerved her round to face him. Leaning forward, he kissed her hard. It was meant as punishment for teasing him, but it was a price she was more than willing to pay.

He cut it agonizingly short and glared at her as he raised his head.

"Eat your food, Green. You'll need your strength to make it up to the chef for that ego-shredding insult."

* * *

The next three days passed in slow, sultry bliss. She sunbathed in the solarium before the midday sun flared too hot. Later in the afternoon, she listened to music on her iPhone or caught up with her emails while Zach swam, a ritual she was learning he repeated twice a day for almost an hour each time.

After the first time she'd seen him walk indoors, droplets of water clinging to his skin and his thick cock firmly outlined in his trunks, she'd given up pretending not to stare.

She squirmed now as she heard him turn on the shower after his swim. No matter how many times they'd devoured each other, the desperate need for him refused to diminish.

Her nipples peaked beneath her white bikini top as she listened to Pink scream about being a slut.

Welcome to my world, sister.

She didn't even need to be in the same room as Zachary Savage in order to hit the state of wet anticipation. And when he walked in with that sure, sexy stride and his eyes zeroed in on her, like they did now, she knew squeezing her thighs together, to stem the ravenous ache building inside her, was no use.

"Good swim?" she asked, her voice breathy in that slutty way Pink would be proud of.

"Hmm," he murmured, heavy-lidded eyes sliding over her scantily clad body. "But it would've been better with you."

"Nah, I would just slow you down. Or jump you mid-stroke."

"Hmm." Determination flared in his eyes, but he banked it a moment later.

Bethany was thankful that he wasn't pushing her to overcome her fear. It was something she'd lived with for so long, she wasn't sure she would ever get over it, and she was glad Zach was letting it be for now.

As she watched, he slowly peeled off his swimming trunks and kicked them away. "Feel free to jump me now," he offered magnanimously. His thickening cock rose from the silky hair that covered his groin.

One thick vein pulsed underneath the stiff length, and her mouth watered with the anticipation of sliding her tongue over it.

Nervously, she glanced towards the open French doors leading inside. "Aren't... aren't the staff around?"

"Nope, I've given them the day off. We have the whole place to ourselves. All day long." He reached forward and tugged at the bow holding her bikini bottoms together. "Come on, Peaches. Time to work on those tan lines."

Within seconds, he had her gloriously naked. Her favorite brand of sunscreen stood on the table next to her lounger. He grabbed it and tipped the oil into his cupped palm. Slowly, he rubbed his hands together, his gaze drifting heatedly over her body.

Seating himself on the edge of her lounger, he lowered his palms to her stomach. Her sharp intake of breath brought a smile to his lips.

Zach loved the effect he had on her, seemed to crave it, in fact. She only needed to be within arm's length for him to find an excuse to touch her. Not that he needed an excuse. She craved having his hands on her as much as he did.

His caress moved sideways over her waist and down to her hips before drifting back up to glide beneath her breasts. He repeated the motion, over and over, each time sliding close to, but avoiding, her hard nipples.

Desire tore through her, and her hips moved restlessly. A moan rose up in her throat, but Bethany forced it down. She refused to beg. She'd begged too many times since she met Zach Savage. Although she'd had him at her mercy when she'd given him the blow job the day they'd arrived in Marrakech, she'd soon learned that the moment would not be repeated. Sure, she'd given several blow jobs since, but that moment of fractured control had remained elusive.

She forced her hips to still and inhaled deeply to regulate her soaring heart rate. Her skin continued to tingle and arousal bit deep, of course, but she intended to cling to her control for as long as possible.

His gaze slowly narrowed as his hands glided up her shoulders in a smooth, devastating caress. As he moved back down and around her breasts, intense eyes gauged her reaction. When she remained motionless, he went lower, over her stomach to the pelvic bones. He kneaded her flesh, the warmth of his hands sending electric currents along her nerve endings.

Another moan threatened. She swallowed it down. His hands left her body for a moment, but only to drizzle more oil into his palm before he started an even more intensive assault on her thighs. Firm thumbs dug into her skin in erotic circles, each rotation drawing close to her sensitive inner thigh.

He was a whisper away from grazing the outer skin of her sex when she jerked away.

"I'm all done on the front, I think."

She flipped over and was rewarded with a moment's triumph when his breath hissed out. For several seconds, he didn't move. Then she heard the slow glide of his palms rubbing together. He went straight for her ass, as she'd known he would.

Shielded from his probing, electric gaze, she reasserted her slipping control. But even with her eyes clamped shut, she couldn't deny the sizzling arousal that stormed through her body. Pleasure soared higher and higher until she hovered on the brink of bliss.

Bethany was contemplating giving in and pleading for him to take her when his breath brushed her left ear.

"Bravo, Peaches. I think you're ready to visit my toy room."

Her head snapped round, and her gaze collided with his.

Stormy grey eyes regarded her with a mixture of admiration and speculation.

"Excuse me? You were testing me?"

He shook his head. "Not consciously. I like your uninhibited response. But I think we can have even more fun, if you're willing to practice a little bit more restraint."

"And you'll only allow me into this toy room of yours if I don't give in easily?"

"You've always had access to it. I told you about it before we left Paris, but you've shown no interest in it." He shrugged. "You don't have to see it if you don't want to."

She licked dry lips, unsure of where this conversation was going. And whether she wanted to pursue it further. But excitement tingled along her skin, her curiosity piqued.

Fun. That was why she was here. Wasn't it? Being brave enough to grasp the adventure?

"Well, since I've never seen a toy room before, I can't tell you one way or the other."

His eyes gleamed, darkened a touch. "So you'd like to see it?"

She thought for a second and shrugged casually. "Sure. Why not?"

The slow, wicked smile that spread across his face made her self-preservation radar vibrate hard.

He stood to his full length, his erection thick and proud.

Her stomach flipped over as a weakness invaded her bones. She could barely lift her hand when he held out his to her.

"Come."

13

He led her along the long hallway that went past his suite in the west wing of the house.

The thought that she was walking through a veritable palace naked added to the surreal moment.

But she didn't have time to dwell on it. The fingers wrapped around hers gave no room for ambivalence or chickening out. And the excitement escalating through her made it impossible to change her mind.

Zach stopped in front of a large arched door and entered a code in the security panel set into the frame.

The mechanism clicked, and he opened it. Stepping to one side, he gently pushed her into the room.

Bethany hadn't been sure what to expect from a toy room. In her wildest imaginings, she'd expected a replica of the decadent lounges on Zach's airplanes.

She couldn't have been more wrong. When he'd mentioned toys, he'd really meant toys.

Gadgets, large and small, had been arranged around the room, each one more suggestive than the next.

In the middle of the room, a large leather swing, complete with cradle and harness, hung from a sturdy tripod. She'd seen one at a bachelorette party once, but it'd been nowhere near as sophisticated as this one. Mesmerized by the ideas tumbling through her mind, she brushed her fingers over the sleek, cool leather.

"Are you imagining yourself strapped in, Peaches?" Zach whispered in her ear. "Your beautiful body wide open to me as I pound into you?"

Heat from his body caressed her back, and she shivered at the decadent sin in his voice. Her nipples peaked at the thought of enacting that scenario, and desire twisted in her pelvis. She forced herself to breathe through it.

Restraint.

"Hmm, maybe."

With a last caress of the leather, she moved to the next piece of equipment.

The indigo-colored, high-backed chair looked innocuous enough, until a simple press of a switch to the side had her gasping. The dildo that rose from the middle of the seat was black, huge and veined, and so life-like she stepped closer to touch it, only to have her hand firmly grasped.

"You won't be needing that."

She laughed. "Do I detect a hint of jealousy there, lover boy?" she teased.

"No, baby, the only time you get to use that is if I'm too worn out from fucking you to move a single muscle. And I guarantee you, that will never happen."

He led her past a modified gurney fitted with handcuffs and a glass cabinet that held everything from anal beads and nipple clamps to bull whips and cock rings.

"Wow, and here I thought my toy drawer was impressive."

He grinned. "I take pleasure seriously," he said.

"I can tell," she replied. She reached another cabinet labeled "Truth or Dare" and stopped. Inside it were a pack of cards and two items—an exquisitely crafted unisex chastity belt and a black silk blindfold.

Zach stopped beside her and followed her gaze. "Another thing you won't be needing."

"What makes you sure?"

"Because we don't play games. We're way past that."

"But games can be fun, Zach. And having fun was the reason I came on this trip, remember?"

She wasn't sure whether she was reminding herself or him. Somewhere along the way, she'd begun to lose sight of why she'd boarded The Indigo Lounge plane in the first place.

Heck, she'd never even had the chance to experience one single lounge event. And with each day she spent in Zach Savage's sphere of existence, she slipped deeper into unknown territory. Territory where the ground shook beneath her feet at the thought of this trip ending and walking away from it when it did.

Regardless of what he'd said in Paris, this thing between them—this fantasy—had no real shelf life. The worlds they came from were too different for any sort of lasting relationship to work.

Her life was in New York. His was not. And if Chris had taught her anything, it was how easy it was to be fooled by someone you loved even while living in the same city.

Zachary Savage was a sexy, dominant, infinitely charismatic man who had women throwing themselves at him. He also had international business interests that took him all over the globe. The moment he walked away from her until he returned, she would tie herself into knots. Her ability to trust had been whittled down to nothing thanks to Chris.

Was that a life she wanted for herself, even in the short term? Her breath shuddered out, and he turned sharply to face her.

"What's wrong?" he asked, eyes narrowed.

She quickly shook her head. "Nothing. What's that?" She pointed to the last, large item in the room.

It was draped with a black silk cloth and set against the far wall.

Sliding another sizzling smile at her, he pulled her after him until they stood in front of the piece. With a firm tug, he pulled the cloth away.

A St. Andrew's Cross made of steel and leather and easily seven feet tall rested at an angle. Stirrups for hands and feet lay undone, ready for a willing victim to step up and splay themselves for pleasure. Double rivets lined the edges of the cross. Closing her eyes for a second, a shocking image of herself on that cross, her body rubbing against those rivets, flashed through her mind.

A furtive glance at Zach caught his intent gaze on her. The small smile that crossed his lips said he'd read her mind.

"Now, this we can certainly have fun with."

"You mean you can. Don't bother denying it, Savage. I can see you salivating at the thought of holding me captive and having your way with me."

He laughed, and she was helpless to halt the deep, rich sound from reaching under her skin and seducing her. When he curled his hand over her nape and pulled her close, she didn't resist. He rubbed his thumb back and forth over her lips before lowering his head to seal his mouth over hers. When they came up for air several minutes later, they were both breathing hard. "Can you blame me? Discovering varied ways of making you come is becoming my obsession. I simply can't get enough of you, Bethany."

The weakness invading her body wasn't new, unlike the sudden knowledge that she was at serious risk of falling in love with this man.

"So, you wanna pick something out and try it? The cross, maybe?" he murmured against her lips.

She wanted to answer yes so badly, her body shook with the desire. It took every ounce of her control to say, "Maybe later."

His stunned surprise bought her the time she needed. Whirling, she rushed out of the room. She was halfway down the corridor before he caught up with her.

"Bethany?"

"I just need to—"

He caught her wrist and forced her to stop. "What the hell's going on?" The worry in his voice was unmistakable.

She shook her head. "All this, what we're doing... it's way out of my comfort zone."

He frowned. "Isn't that the whole point of what you were doing when we met?"

"Yes. But that doesn't mean I don't get to freak out a little every now and then."

His gaze flicked to the door behind them and back to hers. "And the toy room freaked you out?"

"No. Okay, maybe a little. But right now, I just want to take a little breather."

He inhaled sharply. "A little breather? What exactly does that mean?"

She bit her lip. "No sex. For one day."

"No. Hell, no."

"Zach—"

"Bethany," he growled back. His lips were pinched, and the

lines bracketing his mouth had deepened. "I'll give you whatever you want, except that."

"But that is what I want. I can't think straight when we're like this." She waved a hand between them.

He stepped up, closing the gap between them. He slid both hands around her nape and tipped her head up. "I don't want you thinking straight. I want you as mindless with me as I am with you."

"Zach, this is insane..."

He stared down at her for several seconds before he sighed. "It's not insane, but you win. No sex for the rest of the day."

"Really?" She wasn't sure how to take his capitulation.

Leaning down, he skimmed her mouth with his. "Don't sound so pleased. All you're doing is torturing us both. Unnecessarily. But I guess we can try and occupy our time some other way. Go get dressed. I have an idea of what we can do."

She smiled then quickly straightened her features when he frowned at her glee.

"Umm, anything in particular I should know?"

He shook his head, stepped back and took her hand. "It's a surprise. But you'll need to dress comfortably, preferably in pants. And you're allowed to wear panties. Just this once."

Intrigued, she slowly nodded. They entered his room and he drew to a stop. "What?" she asked.

"I don't think I should be in here. Go shower and get ready. I'll use another bathroom."

Her gaze slid over his mouthwatering body to the rampant erection that hadn't subsided. Desire slammed into her so hard she wondered what she'd been thinking when she'd asked for no sex.

"I... umm..." God, even talking was hard.

His nostrils flared, and he took a step back. "Go, Bethany."

She turned and headed for the shower. She didn't need to glance back to know his eyes were riveted on her ass. The sizzling hot sensation all over her skin was evidence enough.

* * *

Despite being a little pissed off at the no sex stipulation, Zach was glad to get out of the house for a few hours.

Although she'd been the one to give voice to it, the slippery, out-of-control feeling he'd experienced since he'd brought Bethany to Marrakech was escalating quickly. The fact that he wanted to carry on regardless was even more unsettling.

He hadn't felt this unsettled, this helpless, since six years ago. Since... Farrah.

He stiffened at the realization.

Beside him at the back of his SUV, Bethany glanced up at him. "Hey, you giving me the silent treatment?" she teased, although her eyes held a trace of wariness.

He smiled distractedly, still unable to process the single thought blazing across his mind.

Farrah.

The one person he didn't want to think about. Especially not while he was with Bethany.

And yet... he'd brought Bethany here, to the one place guaranteed to make him think about what had happened six years ago. Of all his properties around the world, he'd chosen this one...

Christ, a therapist would have a field day with him.

Soft hands caressed his cheek, bringing him back to the present. He captured Bethany's hand and kissed her knuckles.

Her smile held a tinge of relief, and he realized he'd been mostly silent for the last half hour.

The SUV turned into a dirt road, and a row of Bedouin tents swung into view. He flashed her a return smile.

"Ready for your surprise?"

"Umm, no. I'm not loving that look in your eye there, Savage."

His grin widened, and the ache inside his chest loosened a little. Easing a finger down her cheek, he leaned in close. "I won't let anything bad happen to you, but I can't promise that you won't be thrilled out of your mind."

"Huh. That terrifies me even more."

He laughed as they pulled up to the largest tent. The red and gold structure stood in the middle of the encampment. Several Bedouin natives greeted them and led them inside. Large plump cushions lay scattered on Persian carpets, and unlit Moroccan lamps had been strung up across the highest point of the tent.

The scene looked like something out of a movie, and Zach watched as Bethany took it in.

"Okay, I'm liking it so far, but why do I get the feeling I'm in a holding pattern right before I get Punk'd or something?"

He took her hand and tugged her forward. "Have a little faith, Peaches. If I decided to punk you, you'd never see it coming."

He opened the flap at the other side of the tent and her outraged curse froze on her lips.

She gaped at the mostly white camel that stood gazing back at her from half a dozen feet away. Several more camels were scattered in the enclosure, but her gaze returned to the white one.

It moved forward the same time she did. She jerked in surprise and glanced at Zach. "Can I touch it?" she asked in an awed whisper.

"Sure, go ahead."

She stroked a hand down the animal's neck then pulled her hand back when it swung its head to glare at her.

"Oops, I don't think he liked it."

He laughed. "I think he's eager to get started."

"Get started with what?" she asked, the suspicion in her eyes growing.

Zach nodded to the waiting attendants. The first one stepped forward with the chair-like saddle. At a few sharp words in the Bedouin dialect, the animal folded itself gracefully onto the ground.

Several attendants did the same to their animals as a few more guests drifted out of the various tents.

He heard Bethany's soft gasp. "Umm, I hope this isn't what I think it is."

Behind him, Philip stood with the wide-brimmed hat he'd asked him to bring along. Zach took it and placed it on her head. "It's exactly what you think it is, Peaches. We're going camel racing."

A little while later, Bethany shouted with glee as she trotted past him, her grip tight around the two wooden pommels protruding from the saddle.

For the last half hour, they'd ridden deeper into the desert with fifteen other racers. High and low sand dunes undulated across the russet horizon. Beneath them, the red sand kicked up dust as camel feet pounded across it.

The lead Bedouin rider gave a sharp shout, and the animals picked up speed.

Bethany glanced over at Zach again, and his breath caught at the sheer delight in her face. Before now, he'd only seen that look when they'd fucked. He was fast becoming addicted to that look. Hell, he knew it was why he found it damned hard to keep his hands off her. And why he'd pushed thoughts of returning to the real world farther and farther away.

Despite what he'd boldly claimed in Paris, he'd had serious second thoughts as to whether this thing between them could survive outside the bubble he'd placed them in. Sure, everything he'd claimed he could make happen could probably happen, but even he knew there were forces outside his control.

The same forces that had ripped Farrah away from him.

God, why the hell was he thinking about her today? He gritted his teeth as he acknowledged that on some level he'd used sex with Bethany to smother what being here in Marrakech did to him.

But as much as he refused to think about it, he knew he'd have to confront the real world soon enough. Even if he wanted to stay here indefinitely, which he knew he couldn't, Bethany had a life to return to. A life he craved being part of...

He just needed to come up with a solid plan to make it happen.

"Earth to Savage."

He refocused on the woman who sat atop the white camel, her long hair lifting in the breeze. "Are you enjoying yourself, Peaches?"

"Hell, yeah, I'm loving every minute of it." Her gaze dropped to his mouth, and she licked her lips. The knowledge that she wanted to kiss him made his gut clench as fiery lust tore through him. "Thank you."

"You can thank me properly later," he replied.

Her eyes darkened, and her grip tightened on the saddle. The temptation to lean in and kiss her threatened to overcome him.

The sharp cry of the lead Bedouin rider brought a welcome distraction.

Their eyes met again with a look that made his insides sizzle, then he kicked the flanks of his camel and turned it around.

Having grown more confident with each minute in the saddle, Bethany turned her own mount and lined up with the rest of the racers.

The look she sent him as the race leader raised his pistol was both challenging and exhilarating. At the shot, she dug her heels hard into her mount and sprinted away. Zach let her take the lead, content to bask in her excitement and watch the enticing shape of her ass from directly behind her.

Her determination saw her come second, and he grinned as she whooped with triumph and waved her hat over her head like a conquering marauder.

He brought his camel close to hers. As soon as they dismounted, he tugged her to him.

God, he loved how she felt in his arms. So much so that a thread of fear knifed through his pleasure. But it wasn't nearly enough for him to loosen his hold on her.

"Hey, Peaches," he murmured softly.

"Hey," she responded, sliding her hands around his waist. Her breath washed over his face, and he swallowed hard.

"Are you sore?"

She groaned and moved gingerly. "More than I've ever been in my life."

He gave a low laugh and moved in closer, so his next words wouldn't be overheard. "Hmm, I must not be fucking you right, then."

Her fingers tightened convulsively around his waist. "Damn, only you would take that as a challenge. This is an entirely different soreness, Savage."

God, he even loved it when she called him Savage. He glanced at her full mouth, every cell in his body screaming to taste her. He forced himself to stay still, to be respectful of his surroundings. "Come and have some lunch. Then I'll take you to a place where we'll make things all better."

"Another surprise?"

He nodded. "You'll love this one, too. I promise."

* * *

Bethany emerged from the changing room in the luxury spa, which Zach had brought her to after the camel racing, and smiled at the attendant who handed her a thick robe.

"This way, please."

The attendant led her along a corridor with taupe-colored walls. Short candles ensconced in the walls provided soft romantic lighting. Hypnotic Eastern music played over invisible speakers. Through arched windows, a gentle breeze carried gorgeous scents from the carefully manicured gardens. She sighed as the attendant opened a door and stood aside to let her through.

The room was decorated in gold and silver mosaic tiles and held a massage table. A white curtain had been drawn across the middle of the room, hiding what lay beyond.

Curious, she took a step towards it. She gasped when it slid back and Zach emerged from behind it. The white towel tied around his waist did nothing to hide his virility.

Her heartbeat soared as her gaze slid helplessly over his damp skin. With firm hands on her shoulders, he turned her round and walked her back to the massage table.

"Time for your massage."

He tugged her robe off her shoulders, hung it behind the door and turned the lock before returning to help her onto the table.

"Is it worth me even asking if you're allowed to do this here?"

"Do what? You've instituted a no-sex day, remember? I'm just here to make sure you have the best possible time. Without sex."

The sharp pang of disappointment made her bite her lip as she settled on the table.

He reached across her to grab the bottle containing amber-colored liquid. The flex of his abs and the warmth of his golden skin made her want to retract her no-sex stipulation and jump him right there and then.

But being away from his house, watching him interact with others during the race and lunch, and sitting beside him on what she could probably call their first date had shown her that she wanted Zachary Savage outside of the bedroom, too. She wanted more dates. Wanted to know more about him than what made him hard and how long he could hold on to his control in bed.

To do that, she needed to be able to withstand seeing him like this and not touching. She needed to feel his hands on her and think her way through it. Otherwise sex would be all they would have.

Her breath caught.

What the hell happened to just having fun?

She caught his gaze on her and squeezed her eyes shut. She wasn't ready to answer that question, wasn't ready to acknowledge that something was happening to her that scared the shit out of her.

His hands slid up her midriff, and she fought the slide into insanity.

Was it worth contemplating a future with this man? Her every instinct screamed yes, but her head cautioned against it.

Zach had said in Paris that they wouldn't be over after this trip.

And yet, after a week, she didn't know more than a handful of facts about the man who'd fulfilled every single one of her sexual fantasies.

Falling in love with him—if she allowed herself to fall in love with him—would be like falling in love with a ghost.

"I can hear you thinking, Peaches. You're as stiff as a board. Relax."

She cleared her mind of her troubling thoughts and gave in to the firm, hypnotically soothing massage.

She was drifting away on a blissful sea of pleasure when his hand drifted over her shoulders and fell away.

"You ticked an item on your list you didn't even know you had with the camel racing. How about we conquer something else?"

She slowly opened her eyes. A small smile lifted the corners of his mouth, but his eyes were serious. "What are you talking about?" she asked, her sense of comfort evaporating.

He picked her up off the table and slowly lowered her to her feet. Twining her fingers with his, he led her to the curtain and grasped one end of it.

"Your muscles are still sore. I think a warm bath will work wonders—"

Fear congealed in her gut. "No. The massage and shower was all I needed."

"Bethany..."

"Zach—"

She stopped when he slid the curtain back. The square sunken bath was laid with mosaic tiles like the rest of the room. Steam rose from the water on which floated rose petals, and the scent of eucalyptus oil assailed her senses as she walked in.

But nothing could dissipate her fear as she stared at the water.

Dropping his towel, he faced her.

"Do you trust that I won't let anything happen to you?" he asked, his voice firm and solid.

She shook her head at what he was asking. "Trusting you isn't the issue here, Zach. I just don't think... I can't do it."

"You're letting fear win. You're letting that asshole who hurt you win."

A sliver of anger pierced her fear. "And you're psyching me into doing something I don't want to do. Is that fair?" she whispered.

"No. But I'd rather play a little dirty than let you continue to live with the fear."

He stepped into the water. It only came halfway up his calf.

She glanced up at him in surprise and he lifted one brow. "You think I'd put you in deep water the first time you attempt this?"

"I didn't say I was going to do this."

His fingers tightened around hers. "Be brave. Let me help you do this."

She looked from him to the water. She took a step closer and realized she could just about make out the bottom of the bath. Her heart thumped against her ribs as she forced herself not to think about what had happened to her the last time she'd been near a body of water. But the memory of being submerged, of feeling her lungs burst with the lack of oxygen as strong hands forced her under, was too strong.

With a choked gasp she tried to free herself, to get away from the terrifying feeling.

Zach leapt out of the water and caught her to him. He kissed her temple, then buried his face in her hair and held her tight as shudders raked her body.

"It's okay. We don't have to do this right now, if you don't want to."

She squeezed her eyes shut, but the scent of the bath remained in her nostrils. Holding on to him, she slowly opened her eyes.

For almost ten years, she'd let fear rule her life.

You're letting that asshole who hurt you win.

"Come on, baby. I'm sorry for pushing you to do this." He slid an arm around her waist and turned her towards the showers at the opposite end of the room.

Her feet started to dig in. "Wait."

He stilled but said nothing, grey eyes boring into hers.

"I want to do this."

14

"You sure?" Zach asked.

Bethany glanced at the water, her heart still hammering, then slowly nodded. "I want to try."

The admiration in Zach's smile strengthened her resolve. "Atta girl." Lowering his head, he brushed his mouth across hers then tugged her gently back to the edge of the bath.

"Promise me you won't let me go," she blurted as fear threatened to take over again.

A look passed over his face, but it disappeared before she could accurately decipher it.

"I promise," he said simply, but there was a touch of bleakness in his voice. Had she been less preoccupied with conquering her fear and stepping closer to the edge of the bath, she'd have wondered why.

But he was stepping into the rose-petalled water and turning to face her. "Hold on to me. Get used to the water around your feet before we take it further, okay?"

"Okay," she murmured. She stepped into the bath.

Her fingers convulsed around his biceps as the sensation

sent terror through her body. Desperately, she tried to swallow the fear that wanted to take over.

"Calm down, baby. You're doing really well. Stop thinking about what the water can do to you and think about how it feels on your skin. Describe it to me."

She licked her lips and tried to form the words. "It's warm. Silky." She looked down and saw one petal clinging to her knee. The sight was so innocuous it eased her fear a little. "It smells like heaven."

"Good." He stepped in front of her, his back to the rest of the bath, blocking out most of the water. "Now try lowering yourself into it. You know how deep it is. If it gets to be too much, we'll get out."

Sliding her hands down from his nape, she slowly lowered herself until her knees disappeared under the water. More rose petals clung to her skin, their scent rising higher.

Zach followed suit, kneeling in front of her. Then, without letting go, he drew her body flush into his. "You're doing so well, baby."

His encouragement peeled away another layer of her fear. Meshing her hands with his, she slowly sank back until her ass touched her heels. Water lapped between her legs and just above her waist.

They stayed like that for several minutes before he slowly freed one hand. Reaching for a large foam sponge that sat on the edge of the bath, he washed the massage oils from her body.

The fear hadn't dissipated enough for her to completely relax, but Bethany was no longer a prisoner of her terror.

At least she was coherent enough to watch his face as he washed her.

"Why is this so important to you?" she asked.

He kept quiet for so long she thought he wouldn't answer

her. Then his lids lowered as he followed his hand down her belly to her thighs. "When I was younger, swimming meant everything to me. It was my means of escape."

"Escape from what?"

"From the things I didn't want to face." His gaze captured hers, and the jagged pain she saw in his eyes fractured her breath. "Things I don't want to talk about at the moment. Right now, I just want to take care of you." There was a naked plea in his eyes she didn't have the heart to refuse.

And really, how could she demand anything from him right this moment, when he'd single-handedly taken the fear she'd lived with for so long and compressed it from the super-life-sized monster it'd been to something manageable?

She lifted the hand still meshed with his up to her face and kissed the back of it.

His breath caught, and he watched her for several seconds before he resumed washing her.

"Remember what you said about taking my fear away, Zach?" she asked softly.

He nodded.

"I aim to do the same for you." She saw the hard glint of denial in his eyes and shook her head. "No. You don't get to be the tough guy who takes on the world's troubles but never tackles his own. I don't know how or even if I can help you, but I'm going to try."

"You assume too much, Beth. I don't take on the world's troubles. Just yours. As for my own troubles"—he shrugged—"I've learned to live with them."

Before she could counter that, he shifted round until he was behind her. In silence, he washed her back then lifted her out of the water. He walked over to the cushioned seat where a beautiful tea set had been laid out.

Pouring the menthe tea, he handed her a tiny cup. She cradled the bone china and watched him sip his own. Once again, the message that he didn't want to talk about himself came over loud and clear. Frustration warred with the gratitude for what he'd done for her, and in the end, she bit back the need to push for the answers that were clamoring inside her. For now, at least.

Her gaze slid to the bath and back to him. "Thank you."

"You did it all, Bethany. You mastered your own fear and triumphed."

"We both know that's not true. I would never have been able to do it without your help."

His smile was slow and devastating to her senses. "In that case, I accept your thanks. You can show me your gratitude later."

She smiled in return. "I'm racking up quite the tab there, Savage. You think I'll ever be able to repay this debt?"

"I'm sure you will, Peaches. When the time comes, you just need to put your back into it." He winked and downed the rest of his tea.

He waited until she finished her tea before ringing a bell to summon their attendant.

"What next?" he asked, rising to unlock the door.

"I have a mani-pedi. Or a waxing. Or something." Lethargy wound through her, the result of the soothing tea and the fear-fueled adrenaline leaving her system.

"Stick to the mani-pedi or a facial. You don't need to be waxed."

She couldn't help the laughter that bubbled up. "Is that your inner caveman talking?"

He leaned down and kissed her, a devilish gleam in his eyes, as a knock sounded on the door. "Yes, and I make no apologies for him." He pulled her robe more firmly around her and stepped back. "I'm going to hit the pool. I'll see you in an hour?"

She nodded and went with him to the door. They parted ways at the end of the hallway. She watched him walk away, unable to take her eyes off his stunning body.

Two women wearing tiny robes walked past, then turned to stare at Zach, their naked interest sending a spike of jealousy through her. That he didn't even turn to acknowledge their look in any way made the fists she'd unconsciously clench relax a little, but the anxiety wrapping itself around her heart refused to ease.

Well, Bethany, this is no fun, is it?

The mocking voice couldn't be silenced. Nor could the certainty that she was falling for Zachary Savage be shaken.

The attendant gave a tiny cough, jerking her out of her thoughts.

She sat through her grooming session, barely aware of what was going on as the realization hit home with brutal force.

This thing was no longer casual. And it was going to be as messy as she'd predicted the moment she'd set eyes on Zach.

* * *

"Hey, you're giving me the silent treatment now?" Zach asked as they were driven back home.

He'd asked Philip to take the long route home, and the gentle giant had obliged by driving them along the winding roads, which led up into the Atlas Mountains.

The sun was beginning to set, and Marrakech was spread out in all its red and gold glory beneath them.

"What's wrong, baby?" Zach pressed, the light pressure of his fingers on her chin tugging her gaze to his.

"It's been a fantastic day. But it's also been a little bit overwhelming," she answered truthfully. She was amazed by his compassion and determination to help her overcome her fear. But the knowledge that she was risking her heart on a man who was an enigma to her occupied her thoughts now.

Chris had not been an enigma. He'd been a liar and a cheat. But he too had kept her in the dark, and the result had been devastating. She hadn't known what the man she'd been sharing her bed with had been doing, until he'd dropped the bomb at her feet.

Trouble was, she had a feeling any bomb Zach dropped at her feet would be much more devastating than anything Chris had delivered.

Her heart tripped, and jolted back into rhythm, when he tilted her head back and looked deep into her eyes. That intense, unwavering look made her breath catch.

God, she could so very easily make a big-ass fool of herself over this man… if she hadn't already.

"You don't need to worry about anything else right now, Peaches. I've got you. Understand?"

Her nod was stupidly jerky, and her eyes prickled with unshed tears. She was blinking them away when the SUV slowed to a stop. She glanced out of the window and saw that they'd stopped on a ledge just off the side of the road. Zach alighted and helped her out.

"Why are we stopping?"

"Because you need to see this."

15

He led her to the front of the SUV, leaned back against the hood and positioned her in front of him. For several seconds, she stared at the horizon, unable to determine which aspect of the gorgeous view needed her attention.

She started to turn.

He leaned down and whispered in her ear. "Wait for it. It'll happen any minute now." His breath on her ear sent a shudder through her. One arm tightened around her as he raised the other to point at a spot between two mountains. "Keep your eyes on that spot."

She did. Less than a minute later, the setting sun dropped into it, splashing the snow-capped mountains in silver and orange flames. Slowly, the color spread over the valley and across the city. The scene was so spectacular, so breathtaking, she clasped her hands over her mouth in wonder.

They stood like that for several minutes, until the sun disappeared behind the mountains.

"My God, that was beyond beautiful."

"Yes," he breathed. "It was." The simple agreement made her

glance at him. There was a quiet joy in his face as he stared at the view, but there was also a tinge of sadness and pain in his eyes that made her stomach dip alarmingly.

"You really love being here, but this place also makes you sad," she observed quietly. "Why is that, Zach?"

He immediately stiffened. His arm started to drop but she grasped it and held on.

"Talk to me, Zach. Please. I can't help you if you don't let me in."

His jaw tightened. "Did it occur to you that I don't need your help? I told you from the start, there's nothing important enough to impact what happens between us."

"But this is important, don't you see? I can't see your pain and just ignore it. Just as I can't ignore the fact that even though you didn't want to get on The Indigo Lounge plane, you went ahead and joined the trip anyway. Call me presumptuous, but I think you did that because of me—"

"Yes, I did."

She turned fully in his arms. "But why? What happened? The Indigo Lounge is one of the most successful business ventures of this decade, and yet you've had very little to do with it since its inception."

"I employ highly paid and highly motivated people—"

"Don't give me the company line, Zach. I'm not stupid. There's something about this place that has a hold on you, same as with The Indigo Lounge. You don't have to tell me, but please don't deny that it impacts what's happening between us."

"And what do you think is happening between us?"

"You give and expect me to take without giving back. I'm not wired that way. I need to know that I can give you something worthy in return."

"You do."

She sighed. "I'm not talking about sex, Zach."

"Neither am I." His eyes darkened in the fading light. She held her breath and waited. "Being with you... it helps me," he stated quietly.

Her heart leapt. "Helps you... with what?"

"It just helps, Bethany. Can't we leave it at that?" he whispered fiercely.

She started to shake her head and caught sight of Philip, sitting behind the wheel, his face averted from them, trying to be discreet. But there was no doubt the driver had witnessed their argument.

A glance at Zach told her he knew it too, but there was no hint of embarrassment on his face. It made her wonder just how well Philip knew his boss and how many times he'd had to avert his gaze like this. "I know next to nothing about you, Zach. That has to change."

Grey eyes narrowed. "Is that an ultimatum?"

"It's a simple truth. The sex is great. But I need more. Much more, or this won't work for either of us in the long run." She stopped and swallowed. "Or maybe there won't be a long run for us."

"Bethany..."

"I'm not demanding. Hell, I was the girlfriend who was so trusting and oblivious to what her boyfriend was up to that he had to spell it out, remember? But today you called me brave. You helped me to take hold of my fear and crush it. All I'm asking is that you think about doing the same."

"And if I don't?"

It took a surprising amount of effort just to shrug. "I can't answer that. I'm not an expert on relationships. But I know I won't be content to live in a vacuum forever."

He remained silent for a very long time. Then he nodded. "Understood."

They travelled back home in silence. But all through the journey, his arms surrounded her, with her head tucked under his chin. The furtive glances she cast his way showed his face shadowed with myriad expressions she couldn't decipher.

Whatever demons Zach Savage possessed were raging full force. And although it hurt to think she'd been the one to bring them out in the open, she was glad he wasn't brushing them away. His chest lifted and fell in a jagged shudder as they drove through the gates of his house.

Her fingers fisted in his shirt as she felt his pain. Lacing his fingers through hers, he led them into the house but stopped in the large foyer.

"I need to make some calls. I've neglected a few things since we've been here. I'll catch up with you in a few hours?"

Her heart sank. "Oh, okay," she murmured.

"If you're hungry, just dial the kitchen. They'll rustle up something for you."

She tried to smile despite the vice tightening around her heart. Zach was in full retreat mode. He had no intention of confronting his demons. At least not today. "Don't worry, I'll be fine."

He pulled her to him and planted a hard kiss on her parted lips. Heat immediately engulfed her, but he strode away toward his study.

She stood there, her fingers touching her tingling mouth as he shut the study door behind him. For the first time since she'd met him, Zach had actively, willingly retreated from her.

Trepidation welled up in her gut and grew with each passing second.

Perspective. You need perspective, girl.

Whirling, she flew up the stairs and headed for their suite. Going to her side of the bed, she sank down and grabbed her phone.

Keely answered on the third ring. "Hey, Peaches."

Bethany grimaced. "If I told you I'm terrified of losing a man I barely knew a week ago, would you call me crazy?"

"Nope. I live in constant fear of losing men I've never even met, never mind fucked yet."

She squeezed her eyes shut. "I'm serious, Keel."

A sympathetic sigh echoed down the line. "I know, baby girl. I knew it when we spoke last week. Casual relationships aren't your thing. Was I hoping you'd somehow make an exception this time? Probably. And I most definitely wasn't counting on your no-strings guy being Zachary Savage himself. So I've kinda been waiting for this call." Keely's voice oozed sympathy.

"What should I do? He... he won't talk to me."

"You need to find a way to make him."

"I've tried every way I know how."

"Then try something else. Something that's guaranteed to get his attention. Go for broke, or chalk it up to experience and come home before the hurt gets worse."

Bethany kicked her shoes off and slid into bed. Rubbing her foot on the luxurious coverlet, she sucked in a slow breath. "The only thing that gets his attention is sex." The realization made something in her chest hurt. She rubbed absent-mindedly at the spot just beneath her breastbone and gripped the phone harder.

"Are you sure? You've got him hooked enough for him to send a total stranger flowers and champagne. That might be a billionaire thing to do, but it's certainly not a casual billionaire thing, especially from a guy who values his privacy the way Savage does."

"I don't want to hope, Keel. I'm scared I'll get hurt again."

"That makes total sense. But isn't it better to get hurt now than further down the line when you're even more invested?"

Although she agreed with Keely, Bethany didn't want to admit either scenario.

"And remember, there's absolutely nothing stopping you from getting on a plane and coming home now."

That particular thought made her insides twist with panic and fear. "I don't think I can."

Keely stayed silent for several heartbeats. "Then do what Aunt Keely thoroughly recommends. Go for broke."

Go for broke. Could she do it? And if she couldn't, was she prepared to live with the alternative: that she hadn't tried at all? A shiver of apprehension washed over her. Relaxing deeper into the bed, she turned her face into Zach's pillow and inhaled his familiar heady scent. The idea of never smelling him like this again caused her heart to plummet. Seizing the opportunity to change the subject, she smiled. "Speaking of aunts, how's Auntie Mel doing?"

"She can make a miraculous recovery tomorrow. Or she can get worse. You tell me which you want it to be, and I'll make it happen."

Crap. Keely was too clever by half sometimes. Bethany had called because she needed perspective. Keely was holding up the mirror far too effectively, and Bethany had no choice but to confront what lay ahead.

She bit her lip and passed her free hand over Zach's pillow. She recalled the flash of pain she'd seen in his eyes and her resolve firmed.

"I think Aunt Mel needs to be sick for just a little bit longer."

"That's my girl. Go show him what you're made of."

She didn't get a chance to. Not that night. Because once she'd undressed and brushed her teeth, she decided to call her parents. Being vague as to when she would return took more mental dexterity than she'd bargained for. Drained after the call, she pulled Zach's pillow toward her and wrapped her arms round it.

Within minutes, she was asleep.

* * *

She woke alone the next morning. Zach's side of the bed was cold and looked hardly slept in.

Her heart slammed with fresh panic. Tossing the sheet aside, she pulled on the T-shirt he'd discarded. Having his scent engulf her made her feel a little better, but it also brought home to her just how important Zach Savage had become to her.

Leaving the suite, she went downstairs and headed for his study. The door was ajar. She pushed it open.

He sat behind a massive roll top desk, his fingers flying over his laptop keyboard. The intensely focused look on his face made her pause.

"Morning, Peaches," he greeted her softly without looking up.

The greeting raised her mood a notch, and she breathed a little easier than she had a minute ago. But the ache didn't totally subside. She moved forward and sank into the seat across his desk.

"You wear reading glasses?" Heck, even they were sexy. Black, narrow square rims framed his eyes perfectly and increased his sexiness by at least another thousand degrees.

He stopped typing and looked up. Grey eyes speared hers. Seeing the familiar hunger in them gave her another tiny boost of confidence. Whatever was going on, sex was still very much a live and potent thing between them. "Why does that surprise you?" he asked.

"Because you're inhuman everywhere else. You fuck me like you can fuck forever—"

"I can," he stated with no hint of arrogance.

A tingle started deep in her belly. "But you need glasses to read words on a page?"

He smiled as he plucked them off his face. But when his eyes met hers, they were intensely serious. "My eyes may not be perfect, but when you're in my presence all I see is you, Bethany. Only you. And when it comes to you, my vision is fucking twenty-twenty."

Jesus.

How could he say things like that to her and yet not let her in? "You were gone when I woke up."

"You were sleeping so peacefully, I didn't have the heart to wake you. You were tired after yesterday. I didn't think it was fair to disturb you."

She nodded, and her eyes flicked to his laptop. "And now I'm disturbing you. You looked so serious just now."

"I was trying to get stuff done before you woke up."

"Why?"

He toyed with the handles of his glasses. "Because I want to devote today to what makes you happy." His words, like so many before, spoken without guile or adornment, stunned her. He was making her seriously fall for him.

Hell, who was she kidding? She had fallen hard. She had fallen fast, and there would be no turning back. No matter the consequences. No matter that she knew her heart would break in a billion tiny pieces in the end.

Go for broke. "The only way you can make me unhappy is if you push me away," she said boldly.

His eyes darkened. "I'll try and do better," he said.

Bethany's heart stuttered. Considering she'd expected a firm rejection, this was a step forward. It wasn't a huge step, but it would have to do for now. "That's all I ask. Thank you."

He nodded, but his eyes remained solemn, watchful, as if he was expecting something else.

"What?" she asked.

"You were on the phone for a while last night."

She didn't miss the veiled question. "Yep."

"Everything okay?"

"My Aunt Mel is still sick."

Concern immediately clouded his eyes. He dropped his glasses and rounded the desk to crouch in front of her. "Baby, why didn't you say something?"

She tried to keep a straight face but silent laughter shook her shoulders, escalating when she saw Zach's puzzled look. "I'm sorry, I shouldn't really laugh." She explained the Aunt Mel situation and watched his eyes widen.

"Remind me never to cross your friend."

Her laughter subsided. "Yeah, she can be a bit of a pit bull when the mood takes her."

"I'm glad she's been watching out for you." His hand gripped her bare calves in a firm caress then moved up her legs to her knees.

Her breath caught. "You say that like it's a thing of the past."

His hands slid up her thighs and massaged gently. "I'd love to take an active role in watching out for you now."

Again, emotion sucker-punched her. "It's a two-way street, Zach."

He nodded. "You want to level the playing field a bit. I understand that. And I'll make every effort to reciprocate."

Unable to resist touching him, since it felt like a lifetime since she'd last done so, she raised her hand and slowly slid her fingers through his hair. "I'm glad."

They stayed like that for several minutes. Sure, expert hands slowly parted her thighs and stroked higher. "How do you feel?"

"Physically or emotionally?"

Wariness crept into his eyes, but he didn't withdraw from her. "Either. You can tell me whatever you want, Bethany. You know that."

"Okay. I was... upset when I woke and you weren't there."

"I told you—"

"I know what you said, but that's how I felt. And after what happened yesterday, I guess I'm a little... emotional about everything."

"How can I make you feel better?" he asked.

Her fingers drifted over his ear and touched just beneath his earlobe. His tiny hiss gave an indication of his own state of mind. "Having you this close helps."

"Then I'm not going anywhere, Peaches."

"God, Zach. Is it wrong that I'm this greedy for you?" she whispered raggedly.

"Hell, no. If I wanted you any more than I do, I'd have to be carted off in a fucking straitjacket."

His fingers glided higher and touched her outer sex. They both groaned as sensation of a different nature altered the mood.

"Is that my T-shirt you're wearing, baby?"

She nodded jerkily. His thumb moving up and down her clit made forming words impossible.

"Hmm, I feel a sudden chill coming on. I think I want it back."

Her pout drew his gaze to her mouth. Slowly, she licked her lip and watched his nostrils flare. "What about me? Surely you don't want me to catch a chill?"

"I'll keep you warm," he promised. "Now give it back."

She caught the edges of the T-shirt, pulled it over her head and dropped it on the floor.

"God, you're so fucking beautiful." His thumb continued to caress her, but he pulled back slightly. "Scoot to the edge of the seat for me."

Anticipation thrummed through her as she complied. Bethany couldn't believe it'd been barely twenty-four hours since they'd last made love. It felt like a lifetime.

She gripped the armrests as he parted her thighs wider and his head descended. The trail of kisses down her midriff had her gasping for breath.

Watching his pleasure as his mouth trailed lower was its own aphrodisiac. Hearing him groan as her skin quivered beneath his kisses got her even hotter.

Maybe there was something to this after all. Something that went beyond sex for him. No man could get this turned on purely by sex, could he?

Thoughts flew out of her head at the touch of his tongue against her clit. But a loud trill from his desk rudely interrupted her cry of pleasure.

He jerked then closed his eyes on a pithy curse.

"What?" she demanded hoarsely.

"I'm sorry. I forgot I arranged a videoconference call."

The word "video" had her scrambling to locate the T-shirt.

"Relax, no one's about to see you naked. That I can guarantee." His gaze dropped to her wet sex, and he groaned.

"It's okay," she said, although okay was the last thing she felt right now.

"It's not fucking okay. But since I arranged it, I have to show up." Hard regret entered his eyes as she tugged the T-shirt into place. "Don't go far. We have unfinished business."

16

She showered, dressed in a loose white knee-length dress, had breakfast, then tried to convince herself she wasn't behaving like a love-addled idiot when she chose to wait for Zach in the living room closest to his study.

The sound of his deep muted voice as he conducted phone call after phone call soothed her even as her blood thrummed with the anticipation of taking up where they'd left off earlier.

When two hours passed without his appearance, she retrieved her tablet and accessed the bookmarks she'd saved a couple of weeks ago.

After her last run-in with her boss, Bethany had sent out feelers on a few jobs with interesting prospects.

So far, she'd tolerated Sheena's generally acerbic attitude because she'd been too caught up in licking her wounds after Chris. But the thought of returning to Neon to be Sheena's whipping girl made her feel slightly sick.

She had experienced so much change in her life in just a few short days.

Time to embrace it in all aspects of her life.

She was in the middle of sending her resume to a third highly reputable events organization firm when she heard footsteps.

Her heart skipped several beats, and she started to set her iPad aside. But the smile that began in her heart died a swift death on her lips at the look on Zach's face when he entered the room.

"What's wrong?" she asked.

He'd covered his top half with an indigo shirt but a few top buttons were undone, and his hair looked as if he'd ran his fingers through it several times.

"I have a situation with one of my companies. One of my executives has walked out at a crucial stage of a delicate deal. I have to step in, or everything will go to shit."

"Is there anything I can do?" She started to rise, but he shook his head and pressed her back down with gentle hands. He crouched in front of her just as he'd done in his study.

"I appreciate the offer, but no. I just came out here to apologize for neglecting you. I have to take another call in less than five minutes. After that... hell, I don't know how much time it'll take to straighten things out." Grey eyes held hers, his annoyance and worry clear.

"It's fine, Zach. I'm a big girl, I can keep myself entertained for a while longer."

The worried look in his eyes didn't abate. "Are you sure?"

She nodded despite the urge to cling like a pathetic limpet. "Positive. I have a few things to catch up on myself."

His gaze flicked to her iPad and back to her. "Okay. I'll make it up to you, baby. Promise."

His phone rang and he cursed. Leaning down, he kissed her

for a lingering moment and then rose. "Oh, one more thing. Your birthday next week. Don't make any plans, okay? I have a surprise for you." With another kiss and a regretful smile at her, he strode quickly back out of the room.

Her birthday...

The idea that she would be spending it with Zach pleased her far more than was advisable or healthy. The feeling unsettled her enough to jerk her to her feet.

Unthinking of where she went, she wandered from room to room until she reached the ballroom. She hadn't returned since Zach had brought her here on their first day.

The box containing the ballerina slippers sat on the floor where he'd left it. With trembling fingers, she opened it and took out the exquisite slippers. A shade of deep indigo—the choice of color wasn't lost on her—they fit perfectly when she slid them on and tied the ribbons above her ankle.

Her heart skipping rapidly, she walked across the floor and picked up the remote that controlled the sound system. Flicking through, she made a selection and set the control down.

Soft strains of Yo Yo Ma's Cello Suites by Bach drifted through the air. The familiar music alleviated her anxiety and grounded her.

If it makes you happy, do it...

Zach's voice echoed in her head as if he'd whispered straight into her ears. Heart thundering, she practiced a few warmup moves. Her calves twinged at her first demi-plié, but old habits soon kicked in. Keeping relatively fit had helped her body stay toned and limber enough that she dared to attempt a whirling jump halfway through the Suite.

"Yes!" She grinned and kept going. Even when the grand jeté didn't quite make it, she danced on, a sense of joy bubbling just beneath her skin as she twirled from one end of the room to the other.

* * *

In his study, Zach curbed the snarl clawing its way up his throat and forced himself to listen to yet another executive make excuses.

He knew Bethany was no longer next door. He'd seen a flash of white about an hour ago as she'd wandered past his study door. Every cell in his body yearned to be with her, and the sensation wasn't altogether a pleasant one.

His need for her seemed to be escalating beyond reasonable proportions. Granted, they'd passed reasonable quite a while back, but he'd expected a gradual slowing down of the insane attraction between them. Instead he'd spent most of last night contemplating how to give Bethany what she wanted without losing her.

The sky had turned a light shade of grey before he'd crawled into bed beside her. And still he hadn't come up with a way of letting her into his life and his past without the risk of losing her.

He knew, sooner or later, he'd have to find a way to tell her about Farrah.

That truth couldn't stay hidden forever, especially once they returned to the real world. No matter how discreet he tried to keep their relationship, his life was too interesting to the tabloid media for them to remain a secret item for long.

His team of lawyers had done a good job of burying what happened six years ago. He'd done an even better job, until recently, of burying his emotions even deeper.

Could he risk telling Bethany about it now? Would she

understand? God, most likely she would run as fast and as far away from him as possible.

The very thought made his fingers clench on his armrests.

No way would he let that happen.

"Mr. Savage?"

He refocused on the videoconference screen and raised an eyebrow at the table full of sharply suited men on the other side. "Seventy-five percent is non-negotiable. You tried to hard-ball my previous executive, but the simple truth is my company is supplying aeronautic parts and the manpower to build the planes. The only resource you're providing is the fit-out. The numbers work. Take a minute and work it out. Hell, take five."

They turned away to confer and he sat back in his chair. Reaching for his laptop, he activated the program that brought up the security cameras.

He scrolled through the feed until he saw her.

Zach's breath punched through his chest with enough force to jerk him upright. Completely mesmerized, he stared as Bethany floated across his ballroom floor. He couldn't hear the music, but the flow and grace of her body, and the sheer pleasure on her face, made a shudder pass through him.

Jesus, she danced like a fucking dream.

He realized he'd stopped breathing when his lungs burned. Desperately sucking in air, he watched her raise her arms in a graceful arch above her head. Then, staying in pose, she executed the most perfect arabesque.

Zach gritted his teeth at the swiftness with which his cock hardened. But while that reaction was expected, the feeling in his chest as he watched her slowly froze him in place.

Happiness...

"Mr. Savage."

Dry-mouthed, he continued to stare at the screen, unable to

take his eyes off the figure moving through another series of pirouettes and glides.

Happiness, arousal, pride... Fear. All tossed around inside him, jerking his insides into a thousand knots.

Jaw tight, he acknowledged that something was happening here. Something he didn't have complete control over. For as long as he could remember, even before Farrah had come into his life, he'd been able to control his reactions to women. He called the shots and he never apologized or let things get out of hand.

"Mr. Savage?"

The realization that watching Bethany dance had the power to move him so deeply twisted another knot inside him. A knot made entirely of hopeless longing and deep possessiveness.

He wanted her. More than that, he needed her on a level he'd never needed anyone before. He wanted to claim her on every level. Completely. Immediately.

"Mr. Savage. Sir!"

Wrenching himself from the screen, he looked up. Several pairs of eyes stared at him in varying degrees of puzzlement.

Forcing air into his lungs, he cleared his throat. "Gentlemen, what have you decided?"

"We agree to your terms."

"Excellent. Let's move on to the next thing on the agenda."

He waited until their attention had moved from him before he glanced down at the screen. Whatever music she danced to must have come to an end, because Bethany had sunk into a low, perfect curtsy.

Sweat glistened off her skin, but pure happiness shone from her face.

With not-quite-steady fingers, he slowly shut the laptop, the unshakeable sensation cutting a jagged path through him.

From now on, he wanted to be the one to put that look on her face.

Except he knew that for that to happen he had to unearth parts of his life that could very well drive Bethany away.

* * *

Bethany was still smiling when she emerged from her second shower of the day. It was past seven, and the sun was beginning to turn the sky that breathtaking reddish orange that commanded attention.

Zach hadn't emerged from his study all day, but her lunch had been delivered with a single long-stemmed yellow rose and a note that read *Thinking of you, Peaches.*

She had to hand it to him. He had a way of disarming her with very little effort. As a way of making her heart twist into forgetting that there was a side of him she barely knew, it was very effective.

She'd carried the rose upstairs with her and now inhaled its seductive scent as she opened the double French doors, which led to the balcony. Barefoot, she walked onto the terrace.

Flagstones, still warm from the sun, soothed her feet which throbbed from her balletic exertions. She didn't mind the mild pain. The joy she'd felt from dancing again had been immeasurable.

Her only wish was that Zach had been there to see her.

God. She had it bad. Very, very bad.

She rested one hand on the railing, watched the stunning horizon, and tried not to think too hard of what she'd decided in the shower just now. The more she thought about what she'd do to propel a deeper conversation from Zach, the more she was convinced she'd lost her mind.

Plus, chances were it would backfire horribly.

Go for broke.

As she inhaled deeply, the petals of the rose tickled her nose. Could the man who'd sent her the flower really turn away from her that easily if she demanded more?

This morning, he'd told her he'd try. She could wait until he chose his own moment to bridge the gap between them, or she could help him along.

She needed a slow, steady build. The small smile that curved her mouth eased some of her anxiety. She wasn't fully comfortable with the newfound sexual power she seemed to have over Zachary Savage, but if it could aid in her campaign to get him to open up, she was going for it.

With the sun quickly sliding deeper into the horizon, the automatic lights on the grounds began to flicker on. They glinted over the pool and fountain, casting shimmering colors as the water jetted into the air. Trailing her hand over the rail, Bethany slowly walked to the far end of the terrace.

Looking down, she saw even more shimmering water as the shallow pools were illuminated. Despite what Zach had helped her achieve yesterday, the sight of so much water made her pulse skitter with alarm.

She was about to turn away when the structure caught her attention.

A long slab of pavement dissected one of the shallow pools, ending in a mound of rocks that was set into the far wall of the landscaped garden. To one side of the rocks, a small Bedouin tent had been erected.

Distracted by the water, she hadn't noticed the tent at first glance. She frowned at the unexpected sight but, unable to guess from this distance what the structure could be, she turned away and headed back inside.

The door to the toy room was unlocked. Before she lost her nerve, Bethany quickly entered and headed straight for the object she required.

With a cheeky grin, she slid it on and shrugged her robe back into place just as a sound came from behind her.

Zach stood in the doorway, his eyes riveted on her.

17

"There you are," he said. His voice was deep, assured. And his body was as mesmerizing as the sunset had been several minutes ago.

She swayed toward him.

He caught her in his arms and took her mouth in a deep kiss that went on for an eternity.

She was weak-kneed by the time he raised his head and looked down at her with dark, hungry grey eyes.

"Are you done with work?" she asked, her voice a breathless gush that made her cringe inwardly.

His fingers caressed her cheek, and his other hand curled around her waist, pulling her into his hard body. "For now. Dealing with four CEOs with different agendas has its challenges. We'll see what tomorrow brings."

"You love it, though, don't you? The cut and thrust of it all?" she asked.

His sexy grin held more than a tinge of weariness. "Don't use words like thrust when we're this close, baby. It kinda fries my brain." Her blush made him laugh. "Yes, I guess I love it. I wouldn't do it if it didn't interest me." His fingers trailed along her jaw to curve over her nape.

He kissed her again. The scent of the rose grew stronger and she realized they'd crushed it between their bodies. It fell uselessly to the ground when he pulled back. "I missed you, Peaches."

"I missed you too." She trembled from head to toe with the power he had over her. But the feeling strengthened her resolve to dig deeper into the man who now held her heart.

Catching his nape the same way he'd captured hers, she drew her tongue along his mouth. He groaned but then stepped back. "I'd love nothing more than to take you to bed right now and fuck you until neither of us can move. But we do have time to finish what we started in my study this morning before we— What the fuck are you wearing?" he demanded as his fingers encountered her unique underwear.

"Exactly what you think I'm wearing. You asked me to pick something, didn't you?"

He jerked her robe open and stared in disbelief. "And you decided to pick a fucking chastity belt? Are you out of your mind?"

"On the contrary, I've never been more sane. Besides, why did you have it in your collection if you detest it so much?"

"Because I never thought it would be used against me!"

"Ah."

"'Ah'?" He shook his head and stared down at the locked device as if it was his mortal enemy. "Help me out here, Peaches. I'm clearly missing something. What the hell does 'ah' mean?"

She licked dry lips, suddenly not sure if she'd thought this through enough.

"I'm waiting," he growled.

"I just thought we could, you know, play a game."

"A game?" He spat the word out like it was poison. "I'll play any kind of game you want, beautiful, as soon as you take that goddamn thing off." He tugged at the belt then ran his fingers along the seam, looking for a way in.

"That's not how this works, Zach."

"Jesus, Bethany. This isn't going to end well, you know that, don't you?"

"If you stop thinking about what's in your way for a second, perhaps you'll find it isn't all bad."

He straightened and slowly folded his arms.

Her mouth dried as the force of his implacable will hit her. "Very well. Tell me the rules of this game. The quicker we start, the quicker we'll finish. And I can start punishing you for what you're doing to me now."

"Zachary—"

"No, baby. You don't get to back out now or call me Zachary in that sexy voice to try and get your way. I'll do what you want. Then you'll have to do what I want."

She licked her lips. "I've hidden the key to the belt somewhere in this room. If you find it within five minutes, you can take it off. If you don't, I get to ask you any question I want and you give me a straight answer."

He stiffened, and his eyes narrowed. "This wasn't what we agreed this morning."

She shrugged, and his gaze dropped to her breasts. His jaw clenched hard.

"I know. I just thought I'd help you a little."

"Trust me, Peaches. This isn't helping. In any way." He eyed the belt again, and his mouth firmed. "But I'll play along."

Surprise shot through her. "You will?"

"Don't salivate just yet, baby. I aim to win." He tugged off his

Tag Heuer watch, handed it to her and stepped back. "Tell me when."

Unable to believe that he'd agreed to play along, she stared down at the face of the watch blindly for a few seconds before her brain kicked into gear. When the hand struck twelve, she said, "Go."

He strolled through the room like he had all the time in the world. He peered underneath dildos and anal plugs, checked beneath the rocking cock chair and between the straps of the swing.

She held her breath as four minutes passed. He trailed his fingers over the top of the cabinet as the last minute ticked away.

Turning slowly, his gaze travelled over her. He sauntered closer and just stood in front of her.

"Peaches?"

Her heart jumped into her throat as he reached for her. "No... Zach..."

"Ah." He echoed her earlier response.

Firm hands pulled her into his rock-hard body. Fingers speared her hair in a languorous search as he bent his head and kissed her. Her robe fell from her body and he traced hot hands down her back to the belt.

As his fingers slid underneath the back strap of the chastity belt, she moaned in defeat. He plucked the key from where she'd hidden it between her butt cheeks and stepped back.

"Time?" he asked with a smug grin.

She glanced dazedly at his watch. "Six seconds till time."

He didn't answer. Instead, he stepped to her side where the small lock held the belt in place. Sliding the key in, he turned it with a vicious twist. The action caused the underside of the belt to graze against her core. She moaned at the friction.

His eyes narrowed. "I won. You're not supposed to enjoy this."

"I'm… not."

"Liar."

Flinging the belt away, he picked her up and carried her to the gurney. She'd barely caught her breath before he was parting her thighs.

His tongue on her clit ripped a cry from her throat. Relentlessly, he took her to the edge, then left her there until the impending orgasm had receded.

After a third time, he straightened.

"That's all you're getting for now."

"Zach!"

He silently debated for a moment before he pushed a shaky hand through his hair. "No. You brought this on yourself, baby. You get to suffer as much as I do. Anyway, we have to go or we'll be late for our reservation."

"What reservation?" she husked out.

He walked to a corner of the room and picked up the belt. "The one I arranged as a treat for you, and no… it's not another camel ride, although I assure you, you haven't lived until you ride a camel in the black desert night."

"I think I'll pass that particular treat until my next lifetime. I've heard that scorpions the size of buses come out at night in these parts."

"You have nothing to fear, Bethany. I'll protect you."

She trembled again. He saw it, and his mouth curved slightly with male satisfaction.

Ten minutes later, adorned in the indigo lace dress and trembling with unspent energy, she asked, "So what did you plan?"

"We're going to a show. Of sorts." As they went down the

stairs, she noticed he still had the belt. "Gimme a sec. I need to do something."

She followed him to the kitchen where the open fire used for baking traditional bread roared away. He strode to the fire and threw the belt in.

Shocked laughter bubbled from her chest. "I can't believe you just did that."

"Believe it. Now, let's go and enjoy our show."

* * *

Two hours later, Bethany was rudely introduced to another bout of gut-ripping jealousy. She sat in her cushioned banquet seat at the exclusive restaurant Zachary had brought her to in Gueliz and tried to keep her emotions under control.

An impossible task when the approaching rhythmic jiggles signaled the return of the exotic creature who'd been the source of Bethany's simmering anger for the last hour.

Of the three belly dancers who weaved between the tables, she was the most stunning, with eyes that promised celestial delights and hips that rolled with impossible sensuality.

That she'd made a beeline for Zach the moment she'd seen him had set Bethany's teeth on edge. That he'd made no effort to ignore her every hypnotic move had made Bethany want to slap his face. Hard.

"You're not eating," he observed as the dancer drew closer.

"I'm surprised you noticed."

A frown touched his forehead. "What are you talking about?"

The belly dancer was once again in front of him, swaying and rolling like a cobra to a charmer's tune. "Nothing. Enjoy your show."

His eyebrows rose. "My show?"

The jingling grew almost deafening. Zach turned just as the dancer bent forward and offered him her two bountiful, barely restrained breasts.

Bethany jumped up. "I'm not hungry, Zach. Can we leave, please?"

She didn't wait for his answer. Heels sinking into the plush, carpeted floors, she exited the restaurant and struck off toward the well-lit square.

Zach caught up with her barely a minute later. He didn't speak or try to slow her rapid strides.

She walked into the busy square and came to an abrupt halt. "Sugar. I want sugar."

She looked left and right and headed for the stall that offered what she needed. She eyed the assorted confections and picked one dripping in honey.

Zach's jaw tightened as she reached for her clutch, and he handed over a note before she could. His instruction to the vendor to keep the change brought a deluge of thanks that followed them down the street until they were out of the square.

Bethany munched on the sticky honey sweet, aware of Zach's furtive glances at her as they strolled through another quieter souk.

"Talk to me, Bethany. I don't want this distance between us."

"Oh, so you can feel the distance?"

He snorted. "Are you serious? It's a fucking mile wide."

She threw the last bite in a nearby bin and glared at him. "Well, watching that belly dancer eye-fuck you all night has a way of cooling my ardor."

His eyes widened, and a grin spread slowly across his face. "That's the problem? You're jealous?"

"No need to sound so disgustingly pleased about it." She

whirled away, but he caught her hand and roughly kissed her knuckle.

"Oh, but I am. I'm very, very pleased." His voice was just as rough. Grabbing her ass, he squeezed hard. "I don't even remember what she looks like, Peaches."

"That doesn't make it any better."

"I know what will." He set off down a quiet alley, dragging her behind him.

"Where are we going? Zach, slow down."

"No."

18

The alley grew darker, the wall on both sides soaring four floors high. Normally, she'd have been wary of being in such a dark place, but being with Zach, even when he made her blindingly mad, made her feel safe.

Although safe was the last thing on her mind now as strong, impatient hands lifted her off her feet and slammed her against the wall.

"Zach!"

"Do you know if we're discovered, we'll be thrown in jail for years? Even if you were my wife, we'd still be arrested."

She jerked and tried to push him off. "Zach... no." The thought of Zach being married to anyone, to her, made her senses reel. Things she'd avoided thinking about suddenly tumbled through her head, making her hope, making her dream of a future she had no business dreaming of. She'd known him only a matter of days, for God's sake.

"But the danger makes the anticipation sharper, doesn't it?"

She focused as need slammed into her. His fingers edged up her dress, blazing a trail of fire along her inner thigh.

"We can't..."

"No, we can't. It's forbidden." But he didn't stop. His fingers grazed her panties, found her damp and needy. He swore. "What did I say to you about panties, Peaches?"

"That... I shouldn't wear any?"

"So what's this?"

"You can't have your way all the time. Especially not when you annoy me."

"How annoyed can you be with me when you're already wet for me?"

"My body may be stupid crazy about you, but that doesn't mean you have cart blanche over me."

His heated gaze dropped to her mouth. "I saw you dance today. In my ballroom."

Shock zapped through her, made her freeze long enough for him to kick her legs wider. "You did?"

"Yes," he hissed. "You were exquisite, Peaches. Breathtaking. I've never seen anything more beautiful in my life."

"Oh, Zach. How can I be angry with you and yet melt at your words?" She groaned when he flicked his thumb against her clit.

"You don't have a reason to be angry with me. Or be jealous that I'm looking at another woman. Watching her dance reminded me of this afternoon, how I felt when I watched you dance."

With one quick jerk he ripped her panties off. He quickly stuffed them in his back pocket then lowered his zipper.

The sounds of people moving around crept into the alley. Music blared from speakers in the night market two short streets away.

"How... how did you feel?"

"Like I was watching the purest beauty. That I could die in that moment and be glad to stop breathing."

"God!"

They could be found out any second. But Zach's words, combined with the fiery need clawing through her insides, couldn't be quenched. Nor could she stop Zach's forceful yank on her neckline as he exposed her breasts to this hungry mouth.

With one hand at her throat pinning her to the wall, and the other firmly in possession of her sex, he dropped his head and pulled her nipple into his mouth.

She bit her lip to stop from crying out.

Danger swirled in the sultry night air. It skated over skin, intensifying the sensation as Zach pulled harder on her nipple then laved it with his tongue.

Two fingers slipped inside her wetness, readying her for the thick cock that pressed insistently against her thigh.

She grasped his shoulders as she felt herself slipping down the rough, cooling wall.

"Zachary," she moaned, desire glazing her senses and her voice.

"I don't care if they throw me in jail for public indecency, Bethany. I have to fuck you, right here. Right now," he whispered brokenly. "Lift up your dress for me, baby."

She complied without question. Because, God, she wanted this too. Wanted to feel his thick cock inside her more than she wanted to breath. She needed to feel that he belonged to her on at least some level. More than she wanted the freedom that could be taken away should they be discovered.

Reaching inside his trousers, she freed his cock, heard his groan as she caressed his rigid erection. "Fuck me, Zach. Put your beautiful cock inside me and make me come."

"Shit, Bethany. You're like a drug in my veins. No matter how much I get, I only want more of you."

The way he spoke made a dart of pain hook into her chest.

The pleasure in the confession was strained. In fact, she detected the barest hint of anger.

Pain morphed into pleasure as he parted her thighs and surged into her with one hard lunge.

Her muffled whimper excited him. He slammed back into her and she heard his muted shout of pleasure as he touched her in that place only he seemed to find.

"You drive me to this, Bethany. I ache for you. All the damn time." Again, she heard the banked anger in his voice as he fucked her in the forbidden alley.

He increased his tempo, his hand clamped tightly over her mouth as her cries grew frequent and louder. She couldn't help it.

It was what he did to her. Much too soon, she felt the orgasmic momentum build. She grew wetter, slicker, even as her body tightened with the buildup of sensation.

"Are you close, Peaches?"

She nodded frantically, her hands gripping his broad shoulders. He pumped harder inside her. Merciless teeth bit into the side of her neck, then his tongue soothed the pain, only to repeat it again and again. He hooked one knee around his hip, opening her up even more for his penetration.

Then with a grunt, he slammed into her.

"Now, baby. Come for me now!"

She did. Of course she did. Because this man was so in tune with her body, so in control of her emotions, that he could command an orgasm from her with little more than a few thrusts and potent, sexy words.

As bliss cascaded through her in convulsing waves, he snatched his hand away from her mouth and replaced it with his lips. He swallowed her screams of pleasure, devouring them until they became soft, helpless moans.

She was still shuddering through the last of her climax when he sank his teeth into her shoulder with a muffled "Fuck!"

Helplessly, he pumped his seed into her, hot and hard, filling her up until she felt his semen drip down her inner thighs.

"Zach," she murmured, overcome by the emotions storming through her. She touched the side of his face, expecting him to turn and kiss her palm as he usually did. Instead, he remained still for several seconds, then he pulled out of her.

He stepped back and adjusted his pants. Plucking her panties from his back pocket, he used them to clean her up.

Then in silence, he slid his fingers through hers and led her out of the dark alley.

19

He didn't say another word as he helped her into the car, but he kept his arm around her shoulders and her head tucked beneath his chin as they were driven back home.

Her furtive glances showed his face set in hard lines, his eyes containing a faraway look that made her chest tighten.

"What the hell just happened?" she blurted before she could stop herself.

"We broke the law but didn't get caught," he replied.

"I'm not talking about—"

His grip tightened around her shoulders. "I know. I don't have any answers, Bethany. This is a first for me, too."

She noted that his fingers trembled against her naked skin. It sent a shudder through her to think that whatever was happening affected him just as unnervingly as it did her.

"That's it? We're both just going to flounder without talking about it?"

His sigh held a wealth of weariness. "What do you want me to say? That I don't know what possesses me when we touch? That I crave you beyond reason? You already know that. I want you dripping in sweat, pleading for mercy, and screaming for more when I fuck you. I want you mindless. I want you insane for me. Then I want us to repeat the cycle all over again until one of us passes out."

An icy shiver bumped along her skin. "What I'd like to know is why that makes you unhappy."

"Perhaps because I've never felt like this before. And it scares the crap out of me."

Her breath caught. Pulling back, she looked into his face.

Darkened grey eyes stared deep into hers, letting her see the truth of his words. Her heart beat a tattoo far different and far more soul-shaking than the sex they'd just had against the alley wall.

Zach Savage was baring a little of his soul to her. The knowledge made her reel. "Zach..."

He sucked in a long, slow breath. "I've been your slave since the moment I laid eyes on you. Nothing pleases me more than to see you smile, see you laugh, see you happy. I'm sorry my thoughtlessness tonight made you jealous. But even when I looked at another woman, I was thinking about you. That's what you've done to me, Peaches. And yes, it scares me like nothing ever has before."

That floored her. He said it so simply, so matter-of-factly. But then no one had put her first. Ever. Not when it counted and certainly not like this. And she found it really hard to deal with.

She was still trying when he grabbed her by the waist.

"Now you need to say something before I lose my mind."

"I think I'm falling in love with you," she blurted.

He froze and stared at her, nostrils pinched as he paled slightly. "Jesus..." he finally breathed.

Her heart leapt into her throat. "Is that a good Jesus or a very bad Jesus?"

He shook his head. "It's an I-wasn't-expecting-that Jesus."

Her strangled laughter made him raise an eyebrow at her. "Seriously? You're one of the most dynamic, sexiest men on the planet. You've been the equivalent of a force-ten gale since we met, Zach. I've lost several metaphorical nails hanging on for sheer survival."

He frowned. "What are you talking about?"

She laughed. "Why does the fact that you don't even recognize just how incredible you are surprise me?"

"If you're talking about sex—"

"I'm talking about sex, and I'm talking about the things you say to me, the way you look after me, what you did for me yesterday. Sure, there's a huge amount I want to know, but what I know now makes it easy for me to fall for you."

His eyelids swept down, shielding his expression. "Don't fall too fast, Bethany. I may not live up to your expectations in the long run." The hard, implacable note in his voice triggered naked fear down her spine.

"Why do you say that?"

He shook his head. "There are things about me you don't know, things I can't tell you..."

"You can tell me anything, Zach."

The SUV bumped over a pothole, and he glanced away from her. She watched his profile turn remote as he stared out of the window. Jaw tight, he exhaled harshly and shook his head. "No, I can't. I'd much rather you left me because of something I'm keeping from you than because of something that would make you despise me."

Her breath fractured in her chest. "You think whatever you're keeping from me will make me leave you? What did I say to you this morning in your study?"

His lips firmed. “That the only way I’d make you unhappy is to push you away.”

“Yes. And if you’re already anticipating that I’ll leave, then where does that leave us?”

He turned to her again and cradled her face in his hand as the SUV slowed to a stop. “This isn’t a small thing, Bethany. It’s fucking huge and I… I can’t risk it ending us. You mean too much for me to let that happen. And yes, it sounds incredibly selfish, but give us a little more time, baby. Please?”

Her heart pounded long and hard. “I can’t wait forever, Zach.”

He nodded. “I know, and I appreciate that.” Leaning forward, he kissed her with deep reverence. “Thank you.”

They went into the house and headed upstairs. In the shower, he washed her body with the same reverence with which he’d kissed her.

But their hunger for each other raged just as strongly as it had in the alleyway and soon the atmosphere of the simple shower changed to heat and passion. Before her senses flooded with everything that was Zachary Savage, she pulled away.

“Let’s make a deal.”

Suspicion clouded his eyes. “Not if you’re about to try that thing you did with the belt again.”

“How can I? You burned it to a crisp, remember?”

“I remember. But you’ve proven how resourceful you are. Bethany, I’m pretty damn sure I’ll fuck this up in some way before I get some things right. I only ask that you don’t punish me that way.”

The deep hurt in his eyes shocked her.

She touched his face, loved the feel of his rough five o’clock shadow against her palm. “It was less than five minutes, Zach.”

A deep shudder raked through his frame. "It felt like a fucking lifetime."

"Oh, baby." She started to lean down to kiss his lips. Kiss him better. His grip tightened. She raised her gaze to his and saw the determination in his eyes.

He meant to extract the promise from her. Nothing else would satisfy this man who had everything and yet seemed to want her with a passion that swept her clean away every time.

"I promise I'll never keep myself away from you like that ever again."

His massive chest sagged with his relieved exhalation. When he grinned, he looked years younger, and the wicked twinkle in his eyes made her heart catch. "Thank you. It's for your own good, you know?"

"Don't get cocky, Savage. I've just made you a heartfelt promise. Watch your step."

"Yeah, but you never go back on your promises. It's one of the first things I learned about you. And when I said it was for your own good, I meant I saw how withholding yourself from me distressed you, too. That sweet cunt of yours needs constant and careful attention. I need to know that I can give it that attention whenever necessary."

"Oh, what, so all of a sudden you're necessary for me?"

"I'm necessary for you, just as you're necessary for me. The thought of not having access kills me. I need you." He kissed her.

She lived in the world's most cosmopolitan city, yet she'd never met anyone who could create such emotional havoc using only his words the way Zachary Savage could.

"What are you thinking?" he murmured against her mouth.

"I'm thinking we haven't discussed my deal yet."

He pulled back and stared down at her, his eyes suddenly

serious. "I know what you want, and I agree," he blurted as if the words scalded his mouth.

"Really, you agree to reveal one detail about yourself to me every day?"

"You mean like my shoe size or which way I load my junk?" he teased, but the wariness remained.

She slapped his arm and earned herself a quick, hard kiss. "No, I'm pretty sure I know the answer to both of those. I mean, until you're ready to tell me this big thing that could end us, you can tell me things like who your high school crush was, what you did with your first paycheck, that sort of thing."

He switched off the shower, grabbed a towel and wrapped it around her. "Well, today's answer is easy. I didn't have a high school crush."

"Oh," she murmured as she followed him back into the bedroom. "Not even a small one?"

He looked at her over his shoulder and smiled. "Does swimming count?"

She pouted. "No, it doesn't."

"Sorry to disappoint you, baby." He sat on the edge of the bed and beckoned her. "Come here."

Her heart thumped with want and need and—God, *love*—as she went to him. Slowly, he dried her and pulled back the covers. She slid in and he followed.

Their lovemaking was slow, poignant, and so heartbreakingly intense that tears welled in her eyes. He brushed them away, murmuring soft words as he cradled her close. Sighing, she burrowed into him and let his steady heartbeat lull her to sleep.

She woke in the middle of the night, her stomach hollow with anxiety.

Zach's space was empty and cold, just as it had been the day before. Trying hard not to overthink why he'd left their bed in the middle of the night, she slid out and opened the door leading out of the suite.

The hallway lights had been dimmed, and no sound came from any of the rooms. Had Zach taken another business call downstairs?

She went back to the bedroom and slipped on a dressing gown. Seeing that the door to the terrace was ajar, she went to shut it and on impulse stepped outside. Crickets chirped in the warm night and the prevailing scent of exotic spices filled the air. Wrapping her arms around her waist, she breathed in deeply.

As if pulled by some unknown instinct, she retraced her steps along the terrace back to the spot where Zach had found her earlier tonight, staring at the mound of rocks in front of the miniature tent. As she watched, a light came on inside the tent. Her breath locked in her lungs at the familiar shadow outlined against the tent's fabric.

A thousand questions crowded her brain as she stared, unable to tear her gaze away from the scene.

What the hell was he doing out here in the middle of the night?

The anxiety in her belly mushroomed. More than anything, she wanted to storm downstairs and demand answers. She gripped the railing instead.

She'd promised to give him time. He'd agreed to a question a day. Demanding more might push him into clamming up altogether, and that was the last thing she wanted.

The shadow moved, and Bethany stepped back from the railing. Zach emerged into the night air, his head bowed and his posture weighted in a way she'd never seen before. Beneath his white T-shirt his shoulders were tense, and his movements lacked their usual animal grace.

She quickly returned to the bedroom and got back into bed. Heart thundering, she waited. But an hour later, he still hadn't returned.

The thought that he was out there, grappling with whatever demons haunted him, made her leap out of bed again. Opening the door, she was about to head downstairs when the light from underneath the door at the end of the corridor caught her eye.

The toy room.

Mouth dry, she approached and turned the knob.

Zach jerked around and faced her, hand poised midair where he'd been stroking a leather arm band attached to the St Andrew's Cross.

20

"Bethany," he breathed.

Pain radiated from him in waves, hitting her full force. Had she not been holding on to the door knob, she would've reeled backwards.

"Tell me what you need, Zach," she pleaded. "Tell me how to make it better for you."

His harsh exhalation shook his whole body. Haunted eyes locked on hers from across the room, communicating a thousand demands that remained unspoken.

Earlier last night, she'd come up with the plan to use sex to coax Zach into giving her what she needed from him.

Then after the incident in the alley, she'd abandoned the idea of using sex as leverage because she'd believed it would jeopardize everything. Sex was the most precious thing in their relationship. For now.

But she realized she'd didn't have to use sex that way. She could use it to communicate with the man she had fallen for. The man she'd begun to suspect she couldn't live without.

Releasing the door, she nudged it shut.

It was time to give it her all. It was time to go for broke.

She crossed the room until she stood arm's length from him. Slowly, she untied her robe and let it fall to the floor.

His pained exhalation was jagged with threads of deep arousal.

Heart pounding, she reached out and trailed her fingers along his jaw.

"Show me how to make it better, Zachary."

He swallowed hard and shook his head. "I can't. I don't want to lose you."

"You won't lose me. I promise."

"No," he snapped. "Don't make promises you can't keep. I've learned the hard way that nothing lasts forever. You think you're falling in love with me—"

"I don't think. I know. I love you, Zach."

He jerked backward as if he'd been shot. He was pale, and he shook his head, over and over, denying the words that twisted like a live gauntlet between them.

"No. What you feel isn't love. It's just your brain reacting to great sex."

This time it was her turn to jerk. Ice engulfed her, and she dropped her hands from his face. "Don't disparage my feelings."

"I'm stating the facts as I've experienced them."

"As you've experienced them? Don't presume to tell me how I feel."

"Bethany—"

"No. If you don't want my love, that's fine. No, actually, it's not fine. You'll need to come up with a fucking great reason why you don't want it, when every time you look at me, I see how much you want me."

"I do," he rasped. "I want you more than..." He shook his head.

"And I'm here, right in front of you. You don't want me to leave, and yet you try to belittle what I have to give you. What the hell do you want from me, Zach?"

He clenched his fist at his sides, repeating the action from when they'd first met. As if he was denying himself of her. His body burned hers, imprinting his heat on her. "Something I don't have the right to ask."

"Try it anyway."

"I want time. A lot of it. And your belief that no matter what happens, I won't hurt you. Not deliberately."

"And what about my love? What do you want me to do with that?" she asked.

"Use it to stay. Use it to understand when I can't reveal my past to you like an open book."

She trembled at the dark anguish in his voice. More than anything she wanted to step closer, take him in her arms and let the one thing that had always been perfect between them take over.

But she needed more, just a little bit more.

"It's morning, another day. Time for another question."

He shut his eyes, and his head fell back wearily. Without opening them, he nodded.

"When you told me you had no family you wanted to talk about, what did you mean?"

His tension escalated, his biceps bunching under the strain of clenching his fists. "My mother lives in Louisiana. I haven't spoken to her in over ten years."

"Why?"

"Because that was when I accepted that as much as I wanted

to deny it, she would never be who I want her to be," he muttered hoarsely, pain vibrating off his body, hitting her in the gut with the sheer magnitude of it.

"I'm sorry, Zach."

He opened his eyes and the hard, ruthless gleam she saw amid the pain made her breath catch. "Don't be. I knew she was toxic long before I cut her out of my life."

"God, what did she do to you?"

"To me? Nothing. It was what she did to herself. What she let others do to her that was the problem."

"What does that—?"

He stopped her words with one finger across her lips. "No, I've answered your question. Which means the inquisition is over for another twenty-four hours. It also means I have you for another day." His finger slid slowly over her mouth, and she noticed it was trembling. "I need you, Bethany." The naked plea in his voice, in his eyes, made tears clog her throat.

"You have me," she answered simply, hoping that the love vibrating from inside her would heal him even a little.

His breath shuddered out. He lifted her chin with his finger and looked into her eyes. "If I take you tonight, it won't be... I can't promise I won't be a little rough. Are you okay with that?"

Excitement bubbled through the volatile emotions ricocheting in the atmosphere. "I know you won't hurt me."

One arm slid around her, pulling her in to his hard body. "I'll never hurt you, Peaches. Not intentionally."

She nodded, and her gaze flicked to the structure behind him. "But right now you want to tie me to a cross. Am I right?" she asked, her voice husky with deep arousal.

His smile was lopsided, tinged with chagrin. "I'd never given much thought to control or how it would feel to lose mine, until

I met you. Now you touch me and I feel as if I'm losing my mind."

"I feel the same way."

He leaned closer until their foreheads touched. "Today has been… challenging."

"I know."

He turned her around until her back touched the cross. "Give me this. Help ground me a little?"

She shivered at the sensation of the smooth iron studs against her naked skin. Heat flared anew in his face as his gaze dropped to her hardening nipples. His lips parted and his tongue snuck out to rest against his lower lip.

Knowing he was caught helplessly as she was in the same maelstrom of emotion and arousal lent her to the power to take the final step.

Gratitude, wonder, and anticipation blazed across Zachary's face as she slowly held out her hands to him.

He caught and secured her hands above her head, the leather cuffs snug but not too tight. He trailed his fingers down her arm and along her exposed sides, making her squirm with need and a healthy amount of belly-twisting anxiety.

God, she'd strayed so far out her comfort zone, it was beyond ridiculous. But somehow she'd grown to trust Zach, to know nothing would happen here that she didn't want.

"Step up for me, baby." He gave the guttural instruction as he crouched before her, one hand waiting to secure her ankle holster.

Biting her lip, she positioned her feet on the protruding ledge. Quickly, he fastened the cuffs and rose to surge over her.

One forefinger caressed her cheek, his gaze intent on her face. "Tell me how you feel."

"I feel helpless and powerful at the same time," she gasped.

"Perfect. That means you won't give in quickly."

"Give in to what?"

"To this." Lowering his head, he sucked one nipple into his mouth and then bit on the hard nub.

"Zach!" Her cry ripped from her throat as fire flashed through her pelvis. She was soaking wet before he turned to deliver the same attention to her other nipple.

Her hands jerked against her bonds, ramming home how helpless she was. But each tug brought a fresh wave of lust rather than fear.

He started to lift his head. She moaned her protest. "No. More."

The slow, satisfied smile that spread across his face caught at her heartstrings. He repeated the action, closing his eyes to concentrate on his task as she cried out in pleasure.

When he lifted his head, his control was firmly in place.

Zachary Savage was in his element.

The man caught in the riptide of anguish had receded. In his place was the master of sex, whose bedroom skills were honed to perfection.

He suckled her hard, lapped her with lazy sweeps of his tongue until she was poised on the edge of orgasm.

Then he withdrew. Stepping behind her, he brushed her hair to one side and planted hot kisses on her nape.

Reaching around her, he cupped one breast and drifted his other hand down her midriff. He paused at the top of her mound. "Do you want me to touch you here, Peaches?" he whispered in her ear.

"Yes."

"Tell me how wet you are for me first," he instructed hoarsely.

"So wet. I'm dripping with it. I need you, Zach." Her voice caught on a helpless sob.

He shuddered at her back and cupped her almost roughly. "That is your power right there, Bethany. You don't know how much I want to take what you're offering."

"Take it. It's yours."

His head dropped between her shoulder blades, his breath rushing in and out with his harsh inhalations.

"God, Bethany, you don't know what you do to me. Being with you heightens everything, makes me want to grab life by the balls and squeeze every last drop of happiness from it. It's more than I've wanted to do in a very long time. I don't want to hold back. Don't ask me to hold back. I won't. I can't. Not with you."

"I love you," she repeated, because she couldn't not tell him. She couldn't not let him know that he had her. To help him battle his demons. Or at least banish them for a while. "I love you, Zach."

Tears slid down her face. At her back, she heard his gruff sound of pain.

Abruptly, he let her go and strode round to face her.

He gazed at her, eyes filled with turbulent emotion, before he slanted his mouth over hers. His kiss bruised her to the point of pain, his tongue intent on dueling with hers and winning.

When the need for air drove them apart, he permitted her only a second. Then he was back. His hands gripped her in a possessive hold, which she had no doubt would leave marks.

But she didn't care. All she wanted was his thick, veined cock between her legs and Zach so delirious with pleasure that he would forget his pain.

"I love you."

He jerked again at her confession. "Bethany."

"Yes. Please."

He gripped his cock and caressed it from root to tip. Pre-cum dripped at his slit, making hunger claw at her insides. Stepping closer, he took hold of her hips and surged inside with one long thrust.

Their mingled groan echoed around the room. A trembling seized them both as the first wave of pleasure receded a tiny bit. But that was just the calm before the almighty storm, which had been brewing for hours.

His balls slammed against her ass with each hard ram. Despite the ledge giving her a slight height advantage, the power behind his penetration still lifted her off her feet.

Pleasure like she'd never known screamed through her. "Zach," she sobbed, feeling bliss careen closer. He pounded relentlessly, his mouth devouring her wherever he could—her cheeks, her neck, the sensitive underside of her arm.

"Fuck, I... can't get enough of you. Can't..." he gritted out. "Never leave me, Bethany. Please."

"I won't... I won't... Oh, God," she cried out as her orgasm exploded from her core.

"Baby... Peaches." She heard his guttural moan, then he was spewing his load into her, hot bursts of semen that flooded her insides with each body-shaking ripple.

He soothed her body with gentle caresses until their breathing slowed, then reaching up, he released her hands.

Hugging his hot body to her, a sense of peace stole over Bethany. She didn't fool herself into thinking it was a lasting peace, but she grasped it all the same.

When he freed her totally and carried her to the gurney, she didn't protest. He made love to her again on the gurney then strapped her into the swing. By the time he settled her into the gadget-free armchair, she could barely move.

At some point before morning slid into afternoon, then into another angst-filled evening, he picked her up and took her back into their suite and ordered a tray of food to be brought up.

They ate, showered, and got back into bed. There he curled her back into his front and with his arms tight around her, he drifted off to sleep.

21

The sound of his groan woke her. Turning, she held her breath as another groan squeezed through his parted lips.

Zach wasn't caught in a nightmare. But whatever he was dreaming about was vivid enough to evoke a spirited response. He smiled then frowned.

One hand raised as if he was waving, then dropped heavily back down.

Abruptly, he turned away from her.

"Fa..."

She raised her hand to touch him, but he moved again, turning to face her once more.

The blissful smile on his face trapped her breath in her lungs. Again, he raised his hand. This time, his fingers moved in a gentle undulation, as if he was touching something... or someone.

The pain that ripped through her was as irrational as it was impossible to dismiss.

"Zach." As selfish as it sounded, she didn't want him trapped in a dream with someone else when she was right here next to him.

His head jerked but he didn't wake.

"Farrah," he said on a long sigh. "Farrah."

Bethany froze, but her brain buzzed with a hundred thousand thoughts.

Farrah.

She frowned. The name sounded familiar. It was unique enough that she didn't think she'd misunderstood it.

Farrah.

She sucked in a breath as the memory of where she'd seen it blazed in her mind. Ice and a tsunami of foreboding overwhelmed her.

Sliding out of bed, she quickly donned a discarded T-shirt and left the room. It was too early for any of the staff to be up, which was a blessing. She didn't want anyone witnessing her slide into despair and insanity.

She opened the French doors and stepped out onto the terrace. The sight of the shallow and deep pools surrounding the house caused her anxiety to escalate. Forcing it aside, she skirted the building until she reached the long slab of pavement that dissected the shallow pool.

Heart thumping, she fixed her gaze on her target and walked along the pavement to the structure she'd seen Zach emerge from last night.

Up close, she noticed that the rocks had been smoothed into similar oblong shapes. She also saw the thick, multi-colored candle burning to one side, sending the scent of jasmine and eucalyptus into the thin night air.

Her heart rose and fell, her pulse frantically racing as she took a final step closer.

There, inscribed on the largest stone, was the name she'd just heard on the lips of the man she loved. The man whom she'd dared to think could one day belong to her as surely as her heart belonged to him.

Farrah.

"Bethany." Her name was a low imploration. And a hard command.

She whirled.

Zach stood behind her, clad only in the boxers he'd hastily pulled on.

He was so beautiful in the moonlight, so utterly breathtaking. And, she realized with a cold stab of reality, so utterly out of her reach. Still she couldn't look away, couldn't deny her heart one last chance to stop the shattering she knew was coming. "What is this place?" she asked.

He shook his head slowly, his eyes intensely forbidding. "Don't ask, Bethany. Please."

"I can't not," she replied.

His chest rose and fell in a shaky exhalation. And he waited.

"Who is Farrah, Zach?" she asked, although in her heart of hearts, she knew she must be a former lover. Or more.

Bethany remembered seeing her name in a newspaper in Paris. But lumped together with a bunch of other names, she'd had no way of knowing its significance.

Well, she was about to find out.

"Farrah was my wife. We were married for one day. Then I killed her."

* * *

MORE FROM ZARA COX

ABOUT THE AUTHOR

Zara Cox is the writer of spicy contemporary romance, she writes intense, spicy billionaire romances for Boldwood, including the Indigo Lounge series.

Sign up to Zara Cox's mailing list for news, competitions and updates on future books.

Follow Zara on social media here:

- facebook.com/zara.cox.98
- x.com/zcoxbooks
- instagram.com/zaracoxwriter
- bookbub.com/authors/zara-cox

ALSO BY ZARA COX

The Indigo Lounge Series

Mile High Addiction

Sky High Obsession